THE LEGEND OF AKIKUMO

DANI HOOTS

Terminology

Gods

Amaterasu: Shinto sun kami. Sister of Susanoo and Tsukuyomi. Her name means "shining in heaven."

Amenonuboko: Spear in Shinto used to create the first land in the Black Sea. Its name means "heavenly jeweled spear."

Hachiman: Kami of war, divination, and culture

Inari: Japanese kami of rice, fertility, tea, sake, and foxes. Inari can be depicted as a male, female, or androgynous. Since they are the kami of rice, they are also the kami of fertility.

Izanagi: Creator kami of Shinto creation legend

Izanami: Sister-wife to Izanagi in the Shinto creation legend

Kami(sama): Japanese Shinto god/goddesses or spirits

Konohanasakuya-hime: Daughter of the mountain kami Ohoyamatsumi and the goddess of Mount Fuji

Kuniumi: Creation legend of Japanese islands. The name means "birth of the country."

Okuninushi: The kami of nation building, agriculture, business, medicine, love, marriage, and fortune. Resides in Izumo and is the ruler over the other kami.

Onogoroshima: First island Izanagi and Izanami created from the rainbow bridge to the heavens

Ryūjin: Dragon god with the power of the ocean

Susanoo: Kami of the sea and storms. He is considered a trickster similar to Loki. He is the younger brother of Amaterasu and Tsukuyomi.

Takamagahara: Dwelling place of heavenly gods

Monsters/Creatures

Harionago: Beautiful woman with thornlike hair that she can control

Jorogumo: A creature that appears like a woman, but also like a spider

Kappa: Green, turtle-like creatures that live in ponds and steal Shirikodama

Kitsune: Fox that can shape-shift into a human. Known as a trickster in many folklore stories.

Kitsune are known to serve Inari.

Kitsunebi: Flames created by kitsune. They can be any color.

Okami: Wolf yokai that are said to protect the mountains

Oomukade: Man-eating centipede creature

Raiju: A thunder beast that can create lightning. It can appear as many different types of animals and creates ball lightning.

Rokurokubi: Creature that appears human other than its long neck

Tengu: Birdlike yokai that are said to have red skin and large noses. They reside on Mount Kurama.

Tsurube-otoshi: Large-headed yokai that drop down from trees and eat humans

Usagi: Literally meaning "rabbit." In this novel it is used for the familiars that serve Okuninushi.

Yajuu: Monster

Yako: Literally means "field fox," but is another term for kitsune who turn evil

Yokai: Supernatural monsters, spirits, and demons in Japanese folklore

Yosuzume: Bird in folklore that is said to be around wolves or yokai

Zenko: Celestial foxes, or kitsune

<u>*Other Terms*</u>

Aburaage: Deep-fried tofu pouch. It is said that kitsune love this treat.

Ani: Older brother

Ara ma: The expression "oh my"

Baka: Meaning, "idiot"

Busu: Ugly woman

Chichi(ue): How one would refer to their father to another person. The suffix (ue) was used in ancient times if one's family was high in stature.

Daimyo: A vassal of the shogun

Fusama: Paper doors in traditional homes that didn't allow light through (compared to shoji)

Geta: toothed wooden sandals

Haha(ue): How one would refer to their mother to another person. The suffix (ue) was used in ancient times if one's family was high in stature.

Hakama: Traditional clothing that contained trousers that tied at the waist and fell to the ankles over a kimono

Haori: Traditional clothing that was similar to a kimono but only came to the hip or thigh

Happi: Traditional straight-sleeved coat normally worn during festivals

Hitatare: Traditional samurai dress consisting of a jacket and trouser-skirt

Hiyoku: Traditional silk robe worn under a kimono

Inarizushi: Aburaage stuffed with rice or other fillings

Itadakimasu: Meaning "thanks for the food." Typically said before a meal.

(o)Kaasan: Mother

Kanji: A system of Japanese writing that uses Chinese characters

Kanpai: Meaning "cheers"

Kataginu: Traditional men's vest with broad, winglike shoulders

Katana: A traditional Japanese sword

Ki: Spirit

Kimono: Traditional Japanese robe. There are many different styles depending on the occasion.

Konyoku: A mixed bath

Kozane: Samurai armor

Kuso: Meaning "shit"

Magatama: An ancient pendant whose shape is still unknown. It was said that the shape represents a soul.

Matcha: Ground green tea

Miasma: Unpleasant or odorous atmosphere

Mochi: Rice cake filled with red bean or other filling

Nagagi: Proper name for a kimono robe

Natto: Fermented soybeans

Obi: A belt or sash used to tie a kimono

Obidome: Obi clip

Obijime: Sash that ties around the obi and through the knot

Ohashori: Cloth of a kimono that is folded under the obi

Ojisan: Uncle

Onsen: A hot spring

Ossan: Meaning "old man"

Otouto: Younger brother

Samurai: Military nobility from the twelfth century to 1870s

Sen to Chihiro no Kamikakushi: A film by Hayao Miyazaki in 2001. English name is *Spirited Away*.

Shirikodama: A hardened ball in the anus that is said to be the human soul

Shoin-zukuri: Residential architecture of the

military in the Azuchi-Momoyama and Edo periods

Shoji: Paper screen doors that are opaque and let in light

Sode: Kimono sleeve

Sugoi: Meaning "sweet or awesome"

Sugure: Magic or illusion

Takoyaki: Japanese snack made of octopus

Tenugi: Handkerchief

Torii: The large wooden gates in front of shrines

(o)Tousan: Father

Waraji: Sandals made of straw rope

Yukata: Casual summer kimono

Honorifics

~**chan**: Female honorific used for friends. Adds a sense of cuteness, so can be for boys by a girl. Only used between people who have known each other for a long time.

~**kun**: Male honorific for those who have known each other for a while, or to someone who is lower in ranking

~**sama**: Highest honorific

~**san**: Most common honorific, equivalent to

Mr., Miss, Ms., Mrs., or Mx.

CHAPTER ONE

Present day—Kyoto

My seven tails dangled off the edge of the red *torii*, swishing back and forth, dancing to the warm summer breeze that flowed through the air. Inhaling deeply, I breathed in the sweet scent of the maple trees. I rubbed the deep blue *magatama* pendant I wore around my neck to pass the time as I awaited my next victim. My ears twitched at the footsteps coming up the path leading up the mountain.

I cocked my head, my long black and red hair tossing

to the side, to peer down at four teenagers giggling as they held two lanterns to light the way. It was well past midnight, so these couples were out on a dare. The warm summer nights caused many teens to come up from the city for what they called a "romantic challenge" among the serene landscape. There were rumors of ghosts playing tricks on this mountain. I had never seen a ghost here, but I had seen my fair share of terrified humans.

This time it was two couples. Usually a larger group showed up, and they would take turns going up the mountain, seeing who would chicken out and come down first. It made no sense to me, but that didn't matter—I enjoyed playing tricks on them either way.

The couples parted ways at the fork, and I followed the boy and girl on the right first. I noted their clothes as human teens were always wearing similar outfits these days. They both wore a blue blazer, but the girl was wearing a green-and-blue plaid skirt while the boy wore blue pants. Both had a green piece of fabric around their necks, but they tied them differently. Why did so many teens want to match clothes? One of the other *kitsune* had explained it was what they wore to school every day, but I didn't believe him. Then again, I didn't care for human culture anyway.

I hopped to the ground, landing silently on my *geta*, which took a lot of skill to do. Normally the wood hitting the concrete made a loud noise. It took me a few years to master, but it was useful, not only for scaring humans but to sneak past Ichika when she was looking for me. She didn't care for my antics, and if it weren't for the fact I was the last kitsune born in Japan, she would have kicked me out by now for quite a few different reasons.

These humans weren't patrons though—they wanted me to terrify them.

I stayed in my natural form—half fox, half human— as it scared the teens the best. If I turned into a fox, they confused me with the other foxes that lived in the forest and would comment on how cute I was. Kids these days. And if I stayed as a human, they wouldn't even care. But when I was half-and-half, they screamed and panicked as they realized the tales of old were true and that the monstrous kitsune exist. Then they would tell their friends, who would decide to go out on the dare days later. The cycle never ended, and I felt as if it were my duty to keep it going.

The girl hung on to the boy's arm as if scared for dear

life, but it was an act. Taking in a deep breath, I noted no scent of fear was coming off either of them. This couple must not have believed the stories their friends had told them about this place. They were playing the part in order to hold on to one another.

These two were in for an enormous surprise.

As silent as an autumn breeze, I followed, watching as the girl kept clinging to the boy's arm, giggling, blind to what was going on around her.

"Don't you think this place is spooky?" the girl asked. "I can't believe Yuki-san was the one who came up with this dare."

"Don't worry—you have nothing to fear with me here. I've been to this shrine many times, and it's not scary."

The boy was full of himself. There were things to fear in these woods as I had lived here all my life. He lied or only visited in the daytime. During the day, the creatures of the shadows, us *yokai*, hid from humans. During the night, however, was a different story.

They used to dread us, and I wasn't sure if the modern ignorance or past fear was better. Now humans expanded, not caring if they were in the yokais' territory, but at least we weren't being persecuted any longer.

I shook my head, pushing away those memories. Humans once hunted me, but now things had changed. I was the predator, and I could seek my revenge by scaring these kids.

"Besides," the boy kept talking. "Yuki-san just suggested this so she could hold on tight to Shigure-kun."

The girl laughed. "Well, I can't say I blame her."

"What? You want to hang on to Shigure-kun as well?"

"No, I meant so I could hang on to you."

I rolled my eyes. The scent of teenage pheromones filled my nose, making me want to vomit. They were way too lovey-dovey for me. I wanted to add a little excitement in their lives and get them to see each other's true selves.

Running around the torii and through the woods, I stood behind the red lacquered wood a few meters in front of them. As they stepped closer, I let my tails appear from behind the torii.

"What's that?" the girl squeaked.

I moved my tails back and forth.

"I think it's just a fox." The boy shrugged. "They are

active in these parts because of the Inari shrine."

"Is it going to hurt us?"

"No. Foxes are harmless. We will scare it away."

I grinned. Although he acted fine, I smelled the tangy fear coming off his body. It tasted as tantalizing as cold sake on a warm summer night.

I hid behind the torii and jumped up on top of it as the kids passed underneath me. They did not understand what horrors stood above them. Such naive creatures.

Leaping forward, torii after torii, I peered down to find the couple starting to calm down. Now for the next part of my plan.

Using my powers, I summoned a small *kitsunebi* to appear in the middle of the pathway.

"Ara ma!" the girl screamed. "What is that light?"

"It's just a firefly."

"During this time of year? That's not possible. It looks like… It looks like a blue flame!"

"I… I don't know."

"Maybe we should turn back…"

The boy shook his head. "No. We are supposed to meet the others at the top of this mountain."

"Text them!"

"But we will lose! It's just an illusion. We should

keep going."

That was my cue. I jumped down, igniting dozens of more little kitsunebi, giving a faint blue light around the couple and me. I smiled, exposing my fangs, and swayed my seven tails.

The boy and girl screamed, and I wasn't sure which one had a higher pitch. They both spun around and started running, no longer arm in arm.

I, however, was much faster than them.

I ran around and stood in front of them, laughing. Screams and cries filled the once silent air as the couple tried to figure out what to do next. They turned to run up the mountain, but I ran in front of them again. This time I surrounded them with my blue kitsunebi so they had nowhere else to go.

They both stopped and fell to the cement, crying in each other's arms. I raised my hand, creating a big kitsunebi. They shut their eyes as tight as possible.

I disappeared, jumped up on the torii, and watched.

It was a pleasant couple of moments until one of them opened an eye to see why I hadn't killed them yet. Scared, they picked themselves up, looking for any sign of me. I gave none. Before anything else could happen, they ran down the mountain, tears still falling from their eyes and fear emanating from them like an aroma coming off a grill. I took a big whiff of it and licked my lips. This was the life.

Now to terrorize the other two.

"Tsuki Ketsueki!" I heard a voice call.

Kuso. I was in trouble now. I straightened my red *kimono* and black *obi* and turned to find Yamato standing under the torii I was on, her nine orange tails swishing every which way. Her auburn hair was pulled back in a bun. To most it appeared as if she dyed it, but it was her natural color. She folded her arms and pursed her lips into a tight line.

"Ichika-sama, what are you doing up?" I jumped to the ground as I gave her my most innocent smile.

"Don't even try, Tsuki-san. You are in a lot of trouble. What did I tell you about messing with our parishioners?"

"But they aren't parishioners—they are here on a dare."

"I don't care. This is sacred land, and we must keep everyone on it safe no matter why they are here. Over a century has passed and you still haven't learned that."

I bowed my head a little as my ears folded down. "I'm sorry, Ichika-sama. I wanted to give those kids a good story to tell their friends."

She sighed as she flipped open her black fan, which was decorated with gold butterflies that matched her formal kimono. She waved it at herself as the summer nights were rather warm this year and because it was the way she dealt with her pent-up rage against me. She stared me straight in the eyes with her own blue eyes.

"I don't know what to do with you, Tsuki-san. We took you in because Akikumo-sama was the one who brought you to us. But that was a long time ago, and you still don't fit in. You are the last kitsune ever to be born. Why don't you behave?"

I said nothing as memories of Akikumo came back to me, causing tears to form in my eyes. I grabbed the magatama and closed my eyes for a moment. It had been over a century since I last saw him. He disappeared without a trace, and I still hadn't forgiven him for that.

"How about you go back to the shrine and get some sleep? Tomorrow I will have a lengthy conversation with Inari-sama. Then you and I will discuss what to do next."

Bowing, I did as she ordered and wondered what I would do without this place. I had never been on my own. I traveled with Akikumo for hundreds of years until he brought me to this place. What would I do if I had to leave?

CHAPTER TWO

July 1336 (Muromachi Period)—Kyoto, Japan

All I saw was red.

The stench of blood saturated the air, making my hands shake. Flames grew larger and larger, and the smoke tried to mask the metallic smell, but I still tasted it. I huddled in a ball, rocking back and forth.

"Tousan… Kaasan…"

Tears fell down my face as I stared at the blood that pooled under my parents' bodies. Blazing pieces of the wooden roof fell next to me, setting the tatami mat on fire. The fire had grown, and I doubted my home could last much longer. The heat caused my eyes to dry up faster than they produced tears.

"Tousan…" I sniffled. "Kaasan…"

The smoke filled the house and I could no longer breathe. I tried to cover my mouth with the sleeve of my red *happi*, but it didn't help. I coughed and coughed. I had to get away from this place. But I couldn't leave my parents here. Maybe someone could help me—maybe someone could save them.

Grabbing my kaasan's arms with my small hands, I yanked and dragged her through the rubble, using my entire strength. It took a while, but I managed to move her through the shoji that led out into the street. Once I was out of the building, I sat on the dirt and sought to catch my breath.

And that's when I noticed my home wasn't the only one burning. The entire row of houses was up in flames, with men and women dashing through the streets, screaming. Men on horses, holding *katanas* and torches, flooded the streets. The bouquet of fear, blood, and smoke overwhelmed my senses.

Turning, I called out to the families I once shared meals with. "Please help! My *chichiue* is still inside!"

No one stopped for me. I grabbed on to one man's happi.

"Please help me!"

He shoved me to the ground. Tears rolled down my face as I rushed back into my home to help my tousan. He was heavier than kaasan, and it took me a while to move him even a meter. I kept struggling though, as I would never have forgiven myself if I didn't at least try.

Slipping on the blood I had smeared on the ground, I fell on top of my tousan's body. I rose to find my happi and hands covered in blood. It felt thick and sticky, and I wished it would all just go away.

"Tousan?"

Tousan's body didn't move. I placed my ear against his wet, sticky chest. I no longer heard his heartbeat.

An enormous chunk of the roof came crashing to the floor next to me, catching tousan's black happi on fire. I tried to grab his wrist and pull him, but my hands were too slippery. I struggled to grab his ankle, but it was no use as I couldn't wrap my hands around him.

"Tousan!"

I couldn't help him now. I hurried out the shoji and dropped to kaasan.

"Kaasan." I rubbed my cheek against hers, trying to

nudge her awake. "Wake up."

Her eyelids fluttered. "Aiko…" Her voice was hoarse.

"I'm here, kaasan." More tears came. "But tousan… he…"

Our home collapsed, and the flames grew. Kaasan turned and saw what happened.

She coughed and placed her hand on my cheek. "Aiko, run. Get out of here before the scent of human blood devours you." She coughed again, her blood splattering my face. "Even I can sense it with this smoke, and…"

Her eyes stopped focusing on me and her arm went limp. I grasped her hand and placed it on my cheek.

"Kaasan… Kaasan!" I started wailing, not wanting to leave my mother's side.

But she said I had to run. Why was that? What did she mean by the scent of human blood devouring me?

No one paused to help me—no one stopped to ask if I was okay. I watched as the woman who used to sneak me treats when my parents traveled up to the shrine ran past me. Why did she not stop to help? Why did she ignore me?

Why did this happen? Why were so many people

running?

I stood up, my clothes soaked with the blood of my parents. Filling my lungs with air, I breathed in the different scents. It was no longer my parents' blood that filled my nostrils. No, I smelled the essence of human fear. The tangy scent filled my mouth, along with the metallic stench of mortal blood. Saliva dripped from my mouth.

Hunger took over my body, and I gave in to the lust.

My fangs sharpened, and my nails lengthened into claws. The *sugure* that hid my ears and tail vanished and my true form unleashed itself—my kitsune form.

My parents always hid our true forms through sugure, and I did not understand how to control it. Now they lay dead in the street and all I saw was red. All I smelled was fear. All I craved was blood.

Snarling, I leaped onto one man on a horse. He screamed as I snapped my jaws at him. Metallic *kozane* armor covered his skin and my attacks failed. The man threw me off of him. I landed on my hands and feet, hissing.

"Yokai!" the man screamed.

More men riding horses gathered around us. They circled me and pulled out bows and arrows. Five men tugged back their bows, and arrows came raining down upon me. I zigzagged through the obstacles, not letting even one arrow touch my skin or fur. A soldier with no helmet caught my eye, and I jumped up at his head. I bit at his neck, warm blood filling my mouth. Before the other humans retaliated, I leaped off him, running as fast as I could through the street with blood dripping off my lips.

"Stop her!"

I ran faster than them, even as just a child. My bloodlust rose, and I possessed no will to stop it. I had never been around this much fear and blood before. I didn't understand what was going on here.

Friends I had grown up with screamed as they pointed at me.

"Yokai! Yokai!"

I was shaking, panting, growling. The sharp rocks and debris in the streets scratched my hands and feet, but it didn't slow me down. The blood only aided the already stained soil, no longer knowing what red went to whom. Bodies littered the pathways, stained crimson, the stench of death engulfing the city. Those who were still alive tried to escape and run. I looked for anyone who would help me get away from the men on horses, but they only stared at me wide-eyed and turned the other way.

These were my friends—why did they shriek and run away from me? Something hard hit my head and body. I shook my head and turned to find my friend Laito-kun holding a rock in his hand. He and I used to play down by the water when our parents showed in the market. His black hair was crusted in blood and dust, and his eyes were red with tears. I hissed, and he ran away, screaming.

It was all their fault. They all deserved to die.

Due to my distraction, the samurai ran at me with their katanas at the ready. As one man slashed at me, I hopped up onto his arm and bolted toward his face. With my claws extended, I ripped away his throat. Blood splattered my face as I smiled. They deserved this. They all deserved this.

The men screamed and slashed away at me with their katanas. Part of one blade hit my shoulder, blood adding to my already soaked happi and kimono. Hissing, I jumped onto the road.

I no longer saw the buildings or forest around me—only the color red. I howled as blood painted the men and women running past me.

"Kill the yokai! Get her!"

Over a dozen men armed with swords and bows and arrows surrounded me. They kept their helmets on and made a barrier so I couldn't escape or attack. I backed up into the wall, my tail up and hissing.

They pointed their arrows at me, ready to shoot. I looked for an escape, but I discovered no way out of there.

When I thought I had lost all hope, a large white figure grabbed me and started running.

"Stop him! He has the yokai!"

I kicked and scratched, trying to get away from the man that held me in his arms. I slashed in every direction when his grip loosened.

"You are a feisty one, aren't you?" a man's voice asked.

With the little freedom I had, I dropped to the ground and darted toward the outskirts of the town. Now that I could focus, I transformed into a full fox and ran as fast as possible. I didn't want to leave my tousan and kaasan, but I had no choice—I had to get out of there.

Glancing back, I discovered a white figure chasing after me. The creature kept up with my speed. Adrenaline pumping, I pushed my legs faster, but it changed nothing. It still followed.

I made my way into the forest that surrounded Kyoto, ducking under branches and jumping over small bushes. I was smaller than whatever chased me, so I had the advantage of getting through tight spots. It didn't seem to matter though, as I heard the creature's steps as it raced after me. I didn't have anywhere to go or anyone to help me. Whatever chased after me would catch up and get me.

But at least I would be with my family.

Plunging down into what I thought would be a path, I found myself trapped between a few boulders and the hillside. I had nowhere to go. I turned to find a large white creature stepping up to me. Moving my tail in front of me, I growled.

The creature was gigantic and looked like me in its face, but it was much larger. His pure white fur glistened in the full moon. His golden eyes stared at me, and I didn't know if it was because he saw me as his prey or if he was studying me. Slowly he transformed into a man. He wore a white-and-gold kimono with a blue happi over it. His long white hair lay gently against his kimono, along with a small blue pendant.

I kept hissing as he bent to my level and reached out

his hand. I bit down on his palm, growling.

"It's okay. I won't harm you."

I tightened my jaw, not trusting what a human said to me. None of the humans I grew up with sought to help me—why would a complete stranger try to comfort me? No one came to my rescue. I was all alone with only myself to save me.

I looked up again at him and realized among his white hair were beast ears. Then it hit me—he had transformed from a wolf. This person wasn't a human. He was a yokai just like me.

Letting his hand go, I licked his wound. No, he didn't taste like the blood of the humans. But he didn't taste like a kitsune either.

"That's better. I know they scared you, and don't worry, I'm not like those humans. I'm like you, except an *okami*."

An okami was a wolf yokai. I curled up in a tight ball. The okami were much stronger than kitsune even if the kitsune possessed all nine of their tails. He could still attack me.

He crouched closer. "I won't hurt you. I wanted to make sure you were fine. Did those men harm you in any way?"

"They hunted me like an animal. I had to defend myself."

Peeking around, I found no way to get out of there without having to get past him. He had me trapped. The okami sat all the way down next to me.

"I know. I saw. How did you end up in Kyoto? Among the battle, no less."

"I… I…" Tears formed in my eyes. "My *hahaue* and *chichiue*… they…"

I transformed back into my half-human form, and the man wrapped his arms around me. I clutched his blue happi and sobbed.

"It's okay. You are safe now. Cry all you want."

It felt like I sat in his arms for hours, letting the tears fall. Now that I found myself away from the town and away from where the smell of blood filled the air, I could process all that had happened. My family was gone. My home was gone.

And no one cared.

When I finally could breathe again, I leaned back and peered up at the okami who had saved my life. His deep amber eyes stared at me with such kindness. I had never seen someone look at me like that before, other than my own parents.

"Why did you save me?"

He smiled and patted my head. "Because you are just a child, and there haven't been any kitsune born in hundreds of years. I didn't want something so special to die like that."

"Who are you?"

"I am called Akikumo. And what about you?"

My name… I couldn't say it. I couldn't remember it without my heart aching. I shook my head. "I… I don't know."

His eyes watched me, and he brushed the crusted hair away from my face. "Well then, how about I give you a name?"

I looked up at him, wide-eyed. "You would do that for me?"

He laughed. "Why not? How about I call you Ketsueki for the color of your hair?"

Tears started to fall down my face again, and Akikumo wrapped his arms around me, letting me cry in his arms once again.

CHAPTER THREE

Present day—Kyoto

Sitting upon the torii, I watched as the patrons came up the mountain to give offerings to Inari, the kami of rice cultivation and prosperity. Now that it was daytime, I knew that the people weren't doing dares like the teens last night. No, all these people came to either pray to the kami or to enjoy the scenery.

My feet and tails dangled down, but none of the humans walking underneath the torii noticed. I used sugure—a glamour magic that made it so the humans couldn't see me. Learning how to use such magic took me a long time, but I got the hang of it. It helped that humans ignore all things yokai. While they came up here often, giving their thanks to Inari, I noticed the actual belief—the genuine belief—in the supernatural plummeted in the past hundred years. This made it easier to hide from them. Humans can't see what they didn't believe.

Which was why I loved scaring them.

I leaned back and hung backward off the Inari. My long black and red hair dangled down away from my face. None of the humans even noticed. I sighed as I knocked off a black hat a woman was wearing. She jumped and glanced around, trying to figure out why her hat fell to the ground. Before her friends got too much farther, she grabbed her hat and hurried after them. I sighed.

"Hey, Tsuki-san!"

I glanced over to find Daiki standing out in the forest under one of the maples. He wore a smirk on his face as his nine orange tails glistened in the sun. I jumped to the ground and made my way away from the path and toward the trees where he waited, even though I knew no good would come of it.

"What do you want, Daiki-kun?" I asked as I crossed my arms in front of me, careful not to wrinkle the *sode* of my crimson kimono.

His sapphire eyes twinkled. "I heard you got in trouble with Ichika-sama last night. It seems that you have finally gotten yourself kicked out of this place."

News traveled fast in the shrine. I knew it was only a matter of time before the other kitsune started making fun of me for getting into trouble once again. "Ichika-sama hasn't decided yet. I'm waiting for her to finish talking to Inari-sama."

He brushed back his shaggy orange hair with his slender fingers. "How many times has it been now that you have gotten in trouble? If you weren't such a *yako*, maybe you could fit in with us *zenko*."

I narrowed my eyes at him and clenched my fists, my long nails digging into my hand. I knew I couldn't use my kitsunebi on him as too many humans ventured near us. Even if they couldn't see my yokai form, they would be able to see the flames. There was also the fact that Daiki-kun was much older than I was and possessed all nine of his tails.

Although it's not like that had ever stopped me in the past.

"I am not a yako."

"You weren't born in the shrine and never got the proper lessons on how to behave for Inari-sama. The only reason Ichika-sama has kept you around was because Akikumo-sama begged her to adopt you. I'm surprised he didn't pawn you off to someone sooner."

I shoved him. "Take that back!"

He straightened his black *haori* he wore over his white *nagagi*. I wanted to spill *matcha* on his nagagi so he would have to purchase a new one. He enjoyed keeping his clothes in pristine condition.

Two other kitsune peeked their heads from around the trees. Niko and Hikaru. Great, that was all I needed: more people to poke fun at me for getting in trouble last night.

"What's going on here?" Hikaru asked, stroking one of his white-furred tails. He wore a sky-blue nagagi with a white haori on top, which was typical for him. He always seemed to wear some type of blue.

Niko-san scratched her own gray ears with her long pink painted nails that matched her floral kimono. "Causing more trouble, Tsuki-chan?"

The three of them now surrounded me. I knew I couldn't do anything, not without Ichika finding out, and I would be in even more trouble than I already was.

I tried to ignore them and tried to step around Niko-san, but she placed her hand out. "Not so fast."

"I'm glad such an innocent *zenko* as yourself takes the time to harass a *kitsune* like me." I spat. She glared at me with her golden eyes.

"Watch what you say, *yako*. We are your superiors."

"Don't call me a *yako*."

Hikaru leaned back against the maple tree. "Just because that *ossan* raised you doesn't make you respectful. Besides, he's long gone. He just dropped you off here so he could go die in the woods somewhere."

Clenching my fist, I growled. "He's not dead!"

Niko-san's sweet, sarcastic laugh made my ears turn back. "There are no more wolves in Japan. Face the facts. Akikumo-sama is dead."

I punched her straight in the nose. She screamed and placed her hand on her now bleeding nose. Before I could dart into the wilderness, Daiki and Hikaru grabbed me, digging their claws into my wrists.

"We aren't done with you yet!" Daiki bore his claws deeper into my skin, blood dripping down onto the grass.

Niko-san pulled out a *tenugi* with hand-stitched roses on it and wiped the blood away from her face. "You will pay for that, Ketsueki-san."

With her claws extended, she slashed me across the face. Blood trickled down my cheek. Licking my lips, I tasted the metallic liquid.

"Is that the best you can do?"

White kitsunebi formed in her hand. My eyes widened. I didn't expect her to go to such extremes. If I didn't get out of there, I was dead meat. If they did accidentally kill me, they would just use some excuse or hide my body and say I ran away. It wasn't like they cared if I disappeared or not. It was a wonder that they hadn't tried to kill me earlier.

I transformed into my fox form and fell from the grip of Daiki and Hikaru. I bolted into the woods, avoiding the kitsunebi that hit the dirt next to me. I darted under the bushes and zigzagged through the foliage, knowing they weren't quick enough to catch up to me. Over the years, I learned to be a lot faster than them, knowing it was the only way to survive. As long as I got away, they never bothered chasing after me. It was a waste of their efforts.

The blood from the scratches soaked my fur and ran

into my left eye, but I didn't slow down in case they wanted to kill me right then and there. After a few minutes, I found myself on top of the mountain. I was far from where the three bullied me and knew they wouldn't come searching for me way up here. At least not for a while.

I transformed back into my half-human, half-fox form and straightened my red kimono. Noticing I messed up my black obi and golden *obijime*, I sighed. One problem with transforming into my fox form was that when I transformed back, my clothes were always a mess.

I did my best to straighten and tighten my obi and center the *obidome*, even though the *ohashori* didn't look quite right. I knew Ichika would lecture me about keeping my kimono presentable when I was outside my own room. Whatever, it was the least of my problems at the moment.

Jumping up from branch to branch, I made my way to the top of the tree without ripping my kimono. On the highest branch that would still hold my weight, I sat and took a deep breath. The summer air was humid but not as bad as when the typhoons hit. Although it was warm, I loved it as I could sleep here and enjoy the stars. Taking another deep breath, I examined the city's skyline.

Over the years, I had watched this city grow, get destroyed, and grow once again. Never in my seven hundred years had I seen Kyoto like it stood now. Buildings larger than I had ever known possible covered the landscape, and it no longer connected itself to the surrounding nature. Having never left this mountain since Akikumo dropped me off here, I found myself not wanting to deal with the humans. I didn't know how to handle myself around them—not without Akikumo beside me. I didn't trust them. Then again, I didn't get along with the kitsune I found myself around either.

I lay down and stared up at the clouds that glowed from the sun that peeked out. With summer now here, the sun would shine more and the nights would be even warmer. I couldn't wait to spend my days sleeping in the sun and trying to stay out of trouble during the night.

That is, if Inari didn't kick me out of the shrine.

There was nowhere else for me to go. I did not understand where Aki-chan could have gone, and why he never came back for me. The landscape of Japan changed so much in the past century and a half I didn't even know where to start.

Pulling out the magatama, I held it up to the sky. It glowed a deep blue as the sun's light emanated through the stone. It was the only thing I had saved of Akikumo—the only memory I could hold.

A tear escaped my eye and rolled down my cheek. He wasn't dead—there was no way. The other kitsune were jealous I got to explore the rest of Japan without having to comply with the orders of the shrine, more specifically Ichika.

Not a day went by where I didn't miss Akikumo. We spent centuries together, wandering Japan and doing the service of the kami. Why did he disappear? Why had he left me here and never come back?

I would know if he had died. I would have felt it in my heart.

My ears twitched as I heard something walk underneath where I lay. Glancing down, I found Yuki searching around the area. She was Ichika's daughter and was normally sent out to fetch me when Ichika needed something. Rolling over, I dropped from the tree and landed right beside her.

"Eeep!" She jumped, all nine of her orange tails

puffing up more than usual. Even the hair on her ears were sticking straight up into the air. Realizing the noise was me, she took a breath. "Oh, Tsuki-san. You scared me."

"Sorry about that, Yuki-san. I presume your okaasan is looking for me?"

She nodded, her glittering orange hair dancing around her ears. She kept her hair short the entire time I knew her, and such simplicity always made me debate if I should cut my hair again. It was much easier to handle, but then I couldn't style it how Akikumo used to show me how. Somehow my long hair made me feel more connected to him.

I gestured for her to lead the way to the shrine. To the humans, the structure looked like a sizable cement building with black roofing like many other shrines through Japan. Priests and priestesses took care of the shrine, and humans would leave offerings and pray for whatever they needed, whether it be selfish or otherwise. To us yokai, however, the building was much, much different.

Once we went through the last torii, it transferred us yokai into a whole different scenery. Instead of the one building, many buildings made up the area with rooms for each of us kitsune. The principal building, in which the humans laid their offerings, was much larger and housed the Inari. I only set foot in that building once, as they only allowed kitsune who earned all nine of their tails, or other kami, inside. The only time I was allowed in was when Akikumo was visiting and I went to search from him.

Ichika was waiting for me at the entrance, the scowl she usually gave me already formed on her face. Seeing her narrow eyes look at me with such disgust only meant one thing.

She was going to kick me out.

Stepping up to her, I bowed. I kept my head facing the ground, waiting for her to give me my sentence.

She let out a deep breath. "Tsuki-san, Inari-sama would like to speak to you."

My ears perked up and rose. "What?"

She flipped out her sakura-painted fan like she always did when I frustrated her. "It seems Inari-sama wants you to run an errand."

I couldn't believe what I was hearing. I had lived on this mountain for over a century and a half, and Inari now wanted me to speak to them? Not to mention, be given a task after I screwed up for what Ichika deemed "the last time"?

She grabbed the ohashori part of my kimono and straightened it out. "You need to be more presentable to Inari-sama. There, that should do it."

My mouth opened, but no words came out. I never expected this. I glanced over at Yuki-san to find her as surprised as I was. Her eyes were wide and quickly turned bitter. I was going to face some wrath once I was out of my meeting, as it was a great honor for a kitsune to be called upon. Now the "yako" was taking the place of one of them.

"Get to it, Ketsueki-san. Do not keep Inari-sama waiting."

I gave Yuki-san a slight wink and brushed one of my tails against her as I walked past. She scowled, but I didn't let it bother me. The kami had called upon me themself.

CHAPTER FOUR

July 1336 (Muromachi Period)—Hira Mountains

Akikumo never seemed to stop traveling.

It had been days since we left Kyoto behind. There was nothing left to go back to, not after those samurai took over the city. I didn't understand humans and why they would want to destroy the peace that they had. We lived in Kyoto for a couple of years, before we would have to move again. I didn't grow up as fast as most humans since kitsune lived for over a thousand years. We weren't even considered full grown until we were a thousand years old. Then we would have all nine of our tails.

Akikumo didn't have nine tails like my parents did, but he did seem older than them. I watched as he led us through the forest into the mountains. I believed we were north of Kyoto still, but I wasn't good with my sense of direction. I just followed where my mother and father went. And now Akikumo.

We had stopped by a neighboring town that hadn't been attacked by those nasty men on horses, and Akikumo bought me some new clothes. I stayed hidden just outside the town, waiting for him as I didn't want to go near any humans. I waited in the woods, keeping my ears alert and taking in deep breaths. The woods smelled sweet and a little wet from the rain a few nights ago. I liked being out there more than in the towns where it reeked of vile human. The metallic taste of blood still lingered on my tongue from that night.

I heard the crunch of leaves and detected the sandalwood and jasmine scent that Akikumo possessed. I opened my eyes to find him holding a few bags. I jumped up and hugged him.

"Missed me already?"

I blushed and stepped away. Kneeling, he pulled out

two new kimonos and five *hiyoku* to go under the kimonos. The hiyoku were all simple colors, but both the kimonos had patterns of blue flowers across them. One had a white main base color and the other was black.

"These are beautiful. You didn't have to buy me such beautiful kimonos. I would be fine with a simple one."

He shook his head. "Simple won't do if you are traveling with me. We will be meeting many yokai and kami, and I don't want them to think little of you if you aren't wearing a beautiful kimono like they are."

More yokai? I hadn't known many other yokai. My mother and father tried to stay hidden from others like them. I wasn't sure why, as I never asked. I presumed it was so they could blend in with the humans more.

I bowed. "Thank you, Akikumo-sama."

He ruffled my black and red hair. "No need to bow so low. And please, call me Aki-chan."

I couldn't believe he was asking me to call him by such an informal name so soon. I blushed. "Okay, Aki-chan."

"And I will call you Ketsue-chan. Sound good?" He smiled gently and watched me with his golden eyes.

I nodded. "Yes."

He tossed his long white hair back and gathered the sacks he had with him. "Good. Now, can you carry one of these sacks? We have a long road ahead of us before we reach our next stopping point. I have a small home in the mountains north of here. I actually have a lot of homes scattered throughout Japan, but you will learn that later. And you will learn that it is rare for me to be at any one of them for that long of time. Or at least that long of a time for a yokai. We will be staying with a lot of friends and acquaintances. That is, if you want to stay at my side."

I nodded. "I do."

It wasn't like I had anywhere else to go, and Akikumo seemed to be nice enough. I still didn't trust him fully, but I had nowhere to go and he hadn't given me any reason to leave.

"Well then." He turned to the path. "Follow me."

Akikumo wasn't joking when he said we had a ways to travel. We had traveled for two nights now, and I didn't know how much more walking I could do without resting. I carried the small bag he gave me and felt bad that he had three large bags that he carried that included food and clothing for the both of us. He also had a katana at his side, with a light blue, leather-wrapped handle and a gold sheath. I never saw him use it, but I also never saw him take it off. I presumed he was afraid others might attack us, but I had no idea why.

Because humans weren't trustworthy?

Every time I thought about humans, the angrier I became. Those who said they were my friends, those who stayed up at night with me, watching the stars and telling stories—they all betrayed me. They left me to be attacked by the samurai and didn't care that I had almost been killed.

They didn't care that my parents lay dead in the streets.

No, I didn't want to see another human as long as I lived. I wished that they didn't exist in this world so that I could have a peaceful life. The yokai and kami would never treat me like I was just some animal. Aki-chan didn't leave me like the humans did—he saved me from being killed. He didn't even know me, and yet he had shown me more kindness than those who knew me did.

An aching feeling developed in my chest. What was this feeling? I never had known it before that moment, and I didn't like how it festered inside me since the night of the attack.

There was a rustle in the bushes, and Aki-chan quickly pulled out his katana and was at the ready. The blade was a light metallic color, almost as light as Akikumo's hair. I hid behind him, not sure what was going on. Why was he so afraid? Why did he think the noise would bring us harm?

A rabbit jumped out from the bush and hopped off into the distance. Aki-chan let out a breath.

"Nothing to worry about. It was just a little creature."

I let go of his kimono. "Why did you think it would harm us?"

He set down his cloth bags and looked up at the shining sun. "Traveling in Japan isn't safe for those who do it alone. I, of course, have nothing to fear, as yokai wouldn't go against me, but the humans who leave for the woods sometimes become more savage than others. The other humans call them bandits, and they will attack those who try to travel. It is why you don't see many humans traveling, and if they do, they travel from inn to inn in groups to be safe."

So it was humans who were behind his fear. I should have known. They weren't trustworthy, and when they lived out there in nature, where it was serene, they simply turned to violence and attacked those who were just traveling. Every moment that passed, the angrier I got. Tears ran down my cheeks.

Akikumo seemed to notice my face as he knelt down beside me. "What's wrong, Ketsue-chan?"

"Humans. I hate them. They are savage beasts who only know destruction. They don't care about others; they only care about themselves. They have such finite lives—why do they live like this? Why do they not care about taking each other's life? Why don't they just try to help each other instead?"

He wrapped his arms around me. "Oh, Ketsue-chan. Humans are complex creatures. They want to be able to make a difference in the world so that their name will be remembered since they do not live as long as us. There are many temptations and forces that even we don't understand. I believe one day you will though and that you will learn to love humans. They are created by the gods, just like we were."

I shook my head. "No, I will never care for humans. They hurt my family."

Holding me tighter, he placed his forehead on my own. "I know they did, and I'm sorry I couldn't have saved them as well. War is an awful thing. But you are young and you will see many more things before you become a full kitsune."

I didn't know if that made me feel better or not. I didn't want to experience painful things like I had just felt—I wanted to hide and never show my face ever again. I could go on with my life without having to interact with humans again.

But I knew I wanted to be with Akikumo, no matter where he took me. I just had to get used to the life he led. It only had been a few days, but I felt I could trust him.

"Now, should we get going? We are almost there— just a few more hours."

I nodded and he stood up and grabbed the bags. I grabbed my own bag, and we traveled farther into the woods. I noticed that Akikumo would kneel and pick some leaves, then place them in the pouch he had in his white-and-blue kimono.

As he saw me right in his face, he chuckled. "Are you wondering what I am doing?"

I nodded. He took one of the leaves and handed it to me. "Here, try this."

I took it and placed it in my mouth. It tasted cool, pungent, but almost sweet. It was rather delicious, but it didn't explain why he was picking it.

"It tastes good," I said.

"Yes, it is used for tea and a few different medicinal uses. It is called mint. I picked some so we could have some tea tonight."

A drink made of this would taste good. I couldn't wait to try it. Akikumo must have studied plants for a long time because I didn't know any of them. I was too scared that some were poison and had no one to teach me. I wondered who had taught Akikumo.

Those were all questions that went through my mind, but I was still too shy to ask them. I said very little to him, even though he was able to figure out what I was thinking or needing at any moment. I wasn't sure where he came from or how he could read my mind, but he was very good at it.

"Min...t?" I asked, trying to repeat the word he had just taught me.

"Yes, exactly. Come look at this plant."

I stepped closer to him.

He pointed at the stem. "Mint has a square stem, and the leaves are opposite and rotate up the stem, see?"

I nodded, trying to understand what he was explaining. I sort of understood, but I didn't quite know if I would remember.

"And the flowers are small, purple, and group at where the leaves meet the stem. Then if you crush one of the leaves"—he grabbed a leaf and rubbed it with his fingers—"it smells pungent like this."

He held it out for me to take a whiff. It smelled just like it tasted.

"Easy enough?" he asked with a smile.

I nodded. It made sense, and I was sure I could tell from the aroma.

"Now, we better get going. Only a few more days until we reach my place. Are you coming with me?"

I nodded, as I didn't know what else I would do.

He smiled gently. "Good. There is a lot more I would like to teach you."

My tail wagged back and forth as he turned to lead us forward. I wondered what else I could learn.

CHAPTER FIVE

Present Day—Kyoto

I bit at my long nails as I waited on the other side of the *shoji* from where Inari awaited, tasting some of the blood that was left under my nail. Inari handled all their business in this room, including meeting other kami, listening to the prayers of the parishioners, and discussing matters with the kitsune. Akikumo met with them, but I did not attend with him. In all my time here, I talked to Inari once and since then have only seen glimpses of their beauty.

And now Inari wanted to meet with me. I bit some more at my nail, hoping that they wouldn't kick me out like Ichika said they would. Where would I go? What would I do? There was nowhere for me to go, and I understood nothing of the modern world. Everything would have been much simpler if Akikumo hadn't left me here.

I still didn't understand why he left me. Did I do something wrong? Had I caused a little too much trouble everywhere I went? None of the tricks I performed on humans were that dangerous and no one ever got hurt, so why did he leave me here? In his letter he said he wanted me to learn more about my kind and live in a society where I belonged. I learned nothing from them over the decades, other than they held themselves above everyone else and didn't like me. I wondered if I would be like them when I received all nine of my tails. I really hoped not.

The shoji slid open and Ichika-sama motioned for me to enter. I bowed to her and stepped inside the room. The room decor included very simple designs. Shoji panels made up the opposite wall of the room and the side I had just entered from, while simple *fusuma* panels made up the other two walls. A rice field painting decorated one of the fusuma panels. The shoji that faced the outside was left open, letting the natural beauty of the maples add to the scenery. Inari sat at a small table for two that lay in the middle of the room. I knelt to the ground and bowed deeply.

"There is no need to bow that low. Please, take a seat." Inari gestured to the opposite side of the table. Their voice was both sweet yet powerful. They smiled gently, accenting their high cheekbones, and large brown eyes.

I took a seat while still examining them. They sported a short haircut, the modernness surprising me as I didn't expect a kami to follow human trends. Inari also wore a contemporary take of the multilayered kimono with a white plain one with a red obi covered by a pink-and-orange floral kimono that was left open like a haori. It simply hung off them, delicate yet a powerful statement declaring their leadership. Of all the things I hated about the shrine, I very much appreciated everything Inari had done for me. It wasn't their fault that the kitsune picked on me. It wasn't their job to deal with petty squabbles. They had much more to take care of.

"Would you like some tea?" they asked as they grabbed the iron pot.

I slightly bowed my head. "I am not worthy of being served a pot of tea by you, Inari-sama."

"Nonsense. You are my guest today." They poured the tea and handed me the iron cup carved with sakura. I smelled the floral scent of the tea as the steam rose into the air.

I tilted my head down. "Thank you very much." I took a sip and slurped lightly. The strong, earthy flavor with a hint of jasmine filled my mouth. I had never tasted tea so delicate and flavorful, and I had drunk a lot of tea with Akikumo. I stared at it, taken aback. It was the most wonderful tea I had ever had.

Inari laughed a little, seeing my reaction. "It is an excellent tea, is it not? This tea has always been my favorite. Akikumo-sama always tried to get me to tell him where I found it, but I never told him."

"Why is that, Inari-sama?"

"I guess it was to give him something to search for. He and I both have lived for a long time, and it's the petty things that keep us entertained."

I nodded as if I understood, but I didn't, especially since I could have been drinking this tea with him a long time ago. I guess I shouldn't complain, as I had tasted many different, wonderful teas in the past.

"Now." Inari placed their cup down. "Ichika-san has brought up some of the troubles she is having with you."

I lowered my head. "I'm sorry that my disobedience has involved you, Inari-sama. I didn't mean to cause trouble. It was disrespectful to you as you took me in all those years ago. I understand if you want to get rid of me."

"I wouldn't want to get rid of my most interesting kitsune here. No, I understand why you are frustrated, and for that, I am sorry."

I shook my head. "You have no reason to be sorry. You took me in when Akikumo-san brought me here over a century ago. I am truly grateful for everything."

"But you don't believe you fit in, am I right?"

Slowly I nodded. "But that isn't anyone's fault. I wasn't raised with other kitsune, so I don't know how to act or any of the proper etiquette. I acknowledge I have let you down."

"You have not let me down. I am particularly entertained by all the mischief you get into. Between you and me, Ichika-san needs to let loose a little herself. Watching her run after you makes me laugh. But don't tell her I said that."

I smiled. I couldn't believe they found making Ichika run around delightful. A gentle breeze came in from the outside, and some maple leaves danced their way into the room. My shoulders relaxed, and I stopped fiddling with my kimono.

"Now, as to why I brought you here." Inari took a sip of their tea and filled the cup some more. "I believe a lot of your frustration stems from not knowing what has happened to Akikumo-sama, am I right?"

I nodded, a little subconscious that this kami was having to deal with my worries. "Yes."

"As I thought. I think it is time you go on a journey to find what has happened to our friend Akikumo-sama. I am eager to find out myself, if I am being honest."

My heart raced. Was I finally going to be able to find him? Was this when I was going to prove to the others that they were wrong?

"A lot of the other kitsune say he is dead, but I don't believe that. There is no way Akikumo-san could have died without me feeling it."

"I agree. I don't think he is gone." They took a sip of their tea. "And I had a mutual friend of ours recently tell me where they last spotted him."

My ears perked up. "You know where he is?" I asked,

my tails wagging back and forth.

"Yes, but I am not sure if it is correct. They said they saw him about a couple of decades ago, maybe longer knowing yokai, but they have not seen him leave the area. We both assume he is still there."

"He does that sometimes," I explained. "As if he is waiting for something. He will stay in one of his homes and let the time pass until he is needed."

"So I have noticed. Now, would you be willing to go look for him for me? So we both know what has happened to our dear friend?"

I nodded quickly. "Of course. I will do anything to find him."

Inari smiled. "I am glad you put it like that, as there is more to the conditions."

My tail stopped wagging. "What are the conditions?"

Sipping their tea, they continued. "The priest of this temple has a son who I believe one day will be a valuable successor. However, right now he is in high school and is a bit of troublemaker." Inari smiled. "Kind of like you."

"I don't quite understand. Do you want me to scare him or something?"

They shook their head. "No, nothing like that. I want

you to take him with you as you search for Akikumo-sama."

I opened my mouth, but nothing came out. There was no way I could say no. It just wouldn't be an option with a god like Inari, especially when they were giving me the one thing I had always wanted: answers.

"With all due respect," I began. "A human won't be of any help for a yokai or kami matter. Most humans can't even see most yokai these days. I won't be able to protect them from something they can't understand."

"This human can see yokai. That is why I expect he would make a great priest. He will know the surrounding dangers when you are searching, don't worry about that. He also has been training, secretly, how to exorcize the evil yokai. The boy may act like he doesn't care about his father's work, but I can see the things he does when no one is looking. He could become powerful one day. That is, if he has the proper guidance."

"And you assume I am the proper guidance? Wouldn't Ichika-san be better suited?"

"You believe a kami is wrong?"

I lowered my head. "Not at all, Inari-sama. I do not question your actions."

"Good. I trust he will come out of this a lot wiser. And you as well. I know you don't like humans."

My ears twitched. "If you know I don't like humans, then why do you want me to take one with me?"

Inari's amber eyes gently gazed into mine. "Because it is time you learned that not all humans are evil and that we need to learn to coexist. They are not the enemy but a being just like you and me."

"But they are weak-minded and always resort to violence. They act before they think, and they live such brief lives." I listed all the things I hated about humans, then I saw Inari frown. Lowering my head, I apologized. "I'm sorry, Inari-sama. I will do as asked of me."

"I am glad to hear it. Now, let us finish this tea and enjoy the summer day."

I watched as the maples danced around in the wind, the green contrasting the red torii. I rubbed my magatama. This would be my chance to find Akikumo. Taking another sip of my tea, I thought about what Inari had tasked me with. I did not want to take a human with me on this journey, but it didn't appear as if I had a choice.

I just hoped that my terrible luck with humans

wouldn't complicate the mission any further.

CHAPTER SIX

August 1472 (Muromachi Period)—Fukuoka Prefecture, Japan

Time passed since I first started traveling with Akikumo. We spent many years in the Hira Mountains, learning of different plants and of different yokai that live in the region. We even ventured to Mount Kurama once, but the yokai denied me entrance into the main estate since I was a girl. Apparently they didn't allow any women on the top of the mountain. I found the law to be unfair but waited with a few of the outcast *tengu* who lived at the base of the mountain. Since they'd lost their wings, they couldn't ascend the mountain. I pitied them, as they weren't allowed back into their homes where all their family lived. Then again, I had lost my home and family as well. Usually, when Akikumo had business in some of the human cities, I found myself in the wilderness and hoped that no human came across me. I hid somewhere, scared, as I feared he might abandon me for good. But hours later he would come and find me, and we would be on our merry way with some yummy snacks. I didn't want to go back into a human settlement, as I worried what they might do to me if I lost control of my human disguise. No, waiting was much easier.

In the past decade, we ventured all the way to south Japan. I found the summers to be much warmer, which I didn't mind as that meant I didn't need to sleep with a blanket and could enjoy the stars at night. Winter was also a lot less dramatic, unless we found ourselves in the mountains. There seemed to be snow constantly. I stayed in my fox form during those times to keep warm.

The ocean now lay before us and I jumped up and down. Nothing beat cooling off in the ocean. I started to run down the hill toward the water when Akikumo placed his hand on my shoulder.

"Ketsue-chan, not so fast. I have a proposal for you."

Turning, I found the tall okami smiling as he looked down at me with his golden eyes. Akikumo's white hair glistened in the sun, matching his kimono. The top of my head now came up to his chest, as I was a lot taller than I had been a century ago, and I was almost old enough to gain my second tail. I couldn't wait to be that much closer to becoming a full adult kitsune.

"What is it?" I asked, my tail twitching back and forth. We were almost to the ocean, and he decided now was the best time to talk? What was with him?

"We are almost to Hakata, and I need to take care of some business in the town."

"Didn't you visit that town a few years back?"

Akikumo nodded. "I did, but I need to visit again, by orders of Okuninushi-sama. You remember going to Izumo not too long ago, yes?"

"I do. So you want me to stay at the beach while you go to Hakata?" I asked, a little excited to go play in the water.

He shook his head. "Not quite. I want you to accompany me. Your reward for going into the humans' domain will be going to the beach."

I frowned. There was no way I would do that. "But Aki-chan!"

Akikumo knelt down to my level. "Ketsue-chan, you need to learn to forgive the humans and work with them. They aren't all bad. And I will be there, so I promise nothing will happen."

My ears lowered. "No."

"Ketsueki…"

I pouted. "I don't want to interact with humans. They aren't worth the trouble. They don't care about anyone but themselves and always fight. I can live without interacting with one ever again."

Akikumo let out a breath. "Fine. I guess I will eat that *aburaage* all by myself."

My ears perked back up. "Aburaage?"

He nodded. "With *natto* in the middle."

Drool ran down the side of my lip. It had been a while since we had aburaage. The thought that such a delicacy would be available there in a human town surprised me. Usually we only found it in yokai settlements between worlds.

Glancing down at my feet, I whispered, "Well, I mean, if humans can make that food we yokai love, I guess they might be all right."

He laughed. "That's what I thought you would say. Now, should we head to the town?"

I nodded and grabbed his hand as we made our way down the hill. The sea breeze gently caressed my face and played with my hair. The air tasted salty on this summer day, and I could hear birds chirping in the distance. I was thankful no storms were apparent on the horizon as then it wouldn't be as much fun to play in the water.

The town lay in the distance, and Akikumo stopped before we reached the road.

"Now, do you remember how to stay in your human form?"

I nodded and focused on making my ears and tail disappear. Nothing was happening. I looked up at him, eyes wide. "I can't do it!"

He grabbed a leaf from a tree and placed it on my kimono. Suddenly I transformed into a human and I could keep the facade.

"How did you do that?" I asked.

"Some yokai can use leaves to help them transform— a type of sugure. Usually only the younger ones use leaves, so when you get older, you won't have to rely on its power as much. Right now, it's just extra protection so you don't lose your composure. Now, follow me and stay close. If you feel threatened, just tell me and we will leave."

I nodded and followed Akikumo as we came upon the outskirts of the town. A few humans appeared, and I clutched at Akikumo's white kimono, trying to hide myself. What if the leaf fell off? What if it didn't work and I wasn't able to stay appearing as a human and they tried to kill me again? I wasn't ready. Why had he decided at the last minute I would do this?

Probably because he knew I would refuse.

I kept touching my head, making sure my ears were gone. I wasn't used to it as I was in my fox form or my half-fox form most of the time. We practiced human forms occasionally, but I still felt as if I were wearing someone else's skin. It wasn't right.

Akikumo grabbed my hand and smiled down at me. "Everything will be all right. Don't worry."

We entered Hakata, and I gaped at all the people who roamed around. The town was a lot more populous than any town I had visited, although it had been a century. Did humans increase population this quickly? It seemed impossible, yet I was looking at the town with my own two eyes.

At this rate, the humans would take over all of Japan.

"Akikumo-sama, it is good to see you!" A man came up to him, wearing a gray *kataginu* and black *hakama*. He smiled, his teeth all black. I gasped a little, having not seen such a thing in a long while. Yokai never did such things to their body, yet humans were always altering and changing status. I suppose yokai had it easier in understanding the status of other yokai by their power and ki. Humans did not have that luxury.

The man bowed fully to Akikumo, and we did the same in return. After seeing his clothing and teeth, I assumed he was a *daimyo*. Akikumo tried to explain some of the human politics to me while we traveled, but I didn't listen. If I could go on without interacting with humans ever again, I would be a very happy kitsune. But that didn't seem to be the case, as Akikumo was always interacting with humans. Why he did that, I still did not understand. Life was much simpler without them.

"I am glad you are still here, Chikashige-sama. This makes our conversation a lot easier."

He nodded and looked down at me. "Who is this? Is she your daughter?"

I clutched Akikumo's kimono even more and hid

behind him. I didn't like this human examining me. He might notice something was off.

"Something like that, yes. Her name is Tsuki Ketsueki." Akikumo smiled as he turned and forced me in front of him.

The man knelt down. "Later on, how about I treat you to some *mochi*? I believe there is some back at my estate from a meeting I had earlier today."

I smiled. "Really?"

He nodded. "Yes. Maybe even a red bean one is left."

Glancing behind myself, I made sure my tail was still not visible as that was usually when it betrayed my excitement. There was nothing there.

Akikumo placed his hand on my shoulder as the man stood up. "She loves her mochi. I also promised her some aburaage later today."

"I can have some made for her straightaway." Chikashige patted my head. "Especially for a cute child like yours."

I wondered why Akikumo didn't clarify that I wasn't his child, but I supposed it was easier this way. It would explain why I was always with him.

Chikashige's attention turned back to Akikumo. "So, what brings you to Hakata? These are dangerous parts with the wars going on. Kyoto itself has had a war for five years now. The place is almost in ruins."

I couldn't believe what I was hearing. Kyoto was at war? Again? Wasn't there war when Akikumo and I first met? What was with humans—these creatures that had such short lifespans? Why did they waste it with war?

"Chikashige-sama, I came to talk to you about some important information that I bring to each clan leader from Izumo," Akikumo explained. I froze when I heard the word Izumo. It was the location that all the gods traveled to in the tenth month and where Okuninushi resided. He was the kami of nation building, farming, business, and medicine. He was an important god for humans, but he was also the ruler of yokai, spirits, and all things unseen to the humans.

I knew Akikumo attended the festival in Izumo each year with the rest of the gods, but he never mentioned being given information to pass along. He kept a lot to himself, however, when it came to why he traveled and what he did. I never asked questions about it either, as it was never my place. He would tell me when he wanted to.

The human glanced around. "Let us discuss this

somewhere private. Come with me."

He led us through the street where many humans of all different social statures were walking through. I could tell by the teeth but also the dress. I said nothing but kept close to Akikumo, his clothing smelling like the familiar sandalwood and jasmine scent. Anytime I smelled it now, I felt safer and more relaxed. It was almost the scene of what I would consider home, even though we never really stopped moving around. Akikumo did have a home, but we were rarely there.

I looked over at the human, who seemed to know Akikumo. They must have met a few years back when Akikumo visited this village. He didn't stay long, yet this human acted like he was his friend. Could humans really be that trusting?

We entered the dwelling, the scent of a spiced wood filling my nostrils. After spending time learning from Akikumo, I could tell it was cinnamon. It had been a while since I breathed in such a scent. It was rather calming but warming at the same time.

Chikashige led us to the main room and gestured to sit at the table. I followed Akikumo as he sat down in the middle of the *shoin-zukuri*-style room, laying his katana at his side. Chikashige sat down across from us and opened a box. Inside was a mochi.

"Please, Tsuki-san. Take one."

I quickly grabbed it and started to munch on it as the two conversed on matters that didn't concern me. Sweet rice and bean filled my mouth, and I felt as if I were in paradise. I wished I could find mochi more often as it was hard to make and cost a lot. Even in yokai markets it was a prized food. I guess if a human offered me this for nothing in return, I could grow to like them.

"Now." The human put the box away. "Tell me about what you came here for."

Akikumo nodded. "I have been sent by Okuninushi to give you a warning a century to come. There will be visitors from distant lands who will bring stories of a god that doesn't let any other god be worshipped. He wants to make sure your faith will stay loyal to those that have protected you in the past."

Chikashige narrowed his eyes. "People from a distant land? Like the Mongols?"

Akikumo shook his head. "Farther than that. They will come with war in mind, but they want to threaten your relationship with the kami. I have come to warn you to make sure your descendants understand that the kami created you and have protected you for generations upon generations."

Chikashige seemed to ponder this information for a moment. "Why do you think we would turn to their god and leave our own?"

"I am just bringing you the warning that Okuninushi-sama gave me. It is up to you to figure those things out." Akikumo stood up. "Now, I believe I owe my daughter some aburaage. I will be in the market area if you need anything else."

The man stood up and bowed. "Thank you for your help, Akikumo-sama."

Akikumo held out his hand and I grabbed it. With that, he led me into the marketplace where we got to enjoy some aburaage.

CHAPTER SEVEN

Present Day—Kyoto

I glared at the boy who stood in front of me, not that he acknowledged my existence. His brown eyes were glued to his phone as he slid his thumb up and down the screen.

Seriously? Inari thought this kid would be a great priest? His hair was shaggy and bleached, which was rare to see in Japan. I examined his piercings, jeans, and button-down shirt he had open part way and shook my head. There was no way.

"Tsuki-san, are you listening?" Ichika frowned at me. Her face appeared older as she was disguising herself as a human who had served the shrine for a long while. These humans, including the shrine priest, did not know we kitsune existed. I stayed in my normal teen-appearing form, as I didn't show my face to the shrine priests so he wouldn't be suspicious I didn't age. I worked and played behind the scenes.

I nodded. "Yes, Ichika-sama."

"You are to go on this journey to the Hida Mountains for Inari-sama. This is not a vacation, nor is it a time to goof off."

I heard Yamato snicker. I rolled my eyes. "I know."

She handed me the map Inari had made for me to search for Akikumo. "I do not understand why Inari-sama thought you would be the most capable of handling something like this."

Inari told no one what I would really be doing in the Hida Mountains. My guess it was to keep others from mocking me or because they thought Ichika would try to stop it as I might run away to stay with Akikumo once I found him.

Which was exactly my plan.

Then I would just send this delinquent back on a train

and he could report to Ichika for me. Yes, this was going to all go according to plan. I would write an apology letter to Inari and thank them for everything. It would be the right thing to do after all this was over.

"Yamato!" The head priest Hata Mitsue came over. I tried not to laugh at his large black hat. Why did humans who serve the shrines wear those? Ichika scolded me once for stealing one off the head of a priest a few decades back. I thought the entire thing was hilarious, but she disagreed.

"Yes, tousan?" Yamato didn't look away from his phone as he regarded his father. Ichika thought I was bad—this kid was much worse.

"You will treat these women with respect! Ichika-san has served this temple longer than you have been alive!"

Yamato seemed to smile at that comment and put his phone away finally. "I'm sorry, tousan. I will do better."

Mitsue bowed to Ichika and me. "I am sorry for his disrespect. I promise you on this trip he will be on his best behavior."

"As will Tsuki-san."

Yamato and I looked straight at each other. Yeah, both of us knew that wouldn't happen. We both grabbed our backpacks and said goodbye to our two parents. Ichika wasn't actually my mother of course, but that was what we told Mitsue. The story was I was a shrine maiden in training for another shrine and was going on a pilgrimage to strengthen my bond with the kami of Japan. Ichika talked Mitsue into making Yamato take the same pilgrimage as she believed he could be a priest one day. Mitsue never considered his son would take over the Inari shrine, but after much convincing, he agreed to the proposal.

So I was stuck with Yamato for a while. Lucky me.

I stayed in my human disguise, with a simple blue-and-white floral *yukata* as it was summer, and we ventured down the mountain and into Kyoto. Never did I imagine this town could become so huge. The farther we descended the mountain, the thicker the *miasma* of the human city became. I started coughing, a disgusting stench filling my mouth and nose. I almost wanted to vomit from the foul odor. It was like a mix of rotting flesh, valerian root, and horseradish. My nose hairs felt as if they had been burnt and I would never smell fresh air ever again.

Yamato glanced over his phone at me. "Are you all right?"

I nodded. "I'm fine. It's nothing someone like me can't handle."

"You mean a kitsune?" he asked with a slight smirk.

I narrowed my eyes at him. "What makes you say I'm a kitsune."

He laughed. "I can see through your disguise. Also, I've seen you around causing mischief. There are quite a few of you on the mountain, but you are the only one who doesn't have nine tails yet. Then Ichika-san seems to be one of your chief leaders. Her disguise matches how long she has known my father, but it doesn't fool me."

Inari was correct in their assessment about this boy being able to see yokai. He had never interacted with any of us, however, as I would have heard from the other kitsune about it. So even if he'd seen us, he did a great job at hiding it. Did Ichika even know?

"Why don't you tell your father? I would think someone like him would appreciate a son who can see yokai."

He ran his fingers through his dark blond hair. "As if. I have always been able to see yokai, even when I was a child. I used to cry to my haha and chichi, but they never believed me. That's when I learned not to talk about it to anyone. That, and after I started getting picked on at school."

I cocked my head to the side. "Your own parents didn't believe you?"

"Nah. No one does. It's not like they can see the yokai. I don't blame them, as most people don't even believe in all that stuff anymore."

That made no sense to me. Did they not remember all the tales of us? This really was a human-centered world now—a world I wanted no part of.

We made it all the way down the mountain and stood at street level. I coughed some more. This miasma was so thick, how could humans even breath? This stench was sickening.

"Are you sure you are okay?" he asked again.

"I'll be fine. We won't be in the city for long. Besides, we are heading to the mountains where it won't be as bad. So, which way should we start walking?"

"To the train station. Didn't Ichika-san give you train tickets?"

I looked at him, a little confused. "What... what is a train?"

He smacked his hand on his face. "Really? Have you

not left the mountain for that long?"

I nodded. "I have not left the mountain since Aki-chan dropped me off. Without him, I do not understand the point of interacting with humans."

Yamato laughed. "Well, I can't blame you for that. Humans do suck." He scratched the back of his head. "Well, the train station is this way."

I eyed him as we started forward. "Why are you agreeing to all this? You don't seem one to take orders from anyone, whether it be your parents or a kitsune."

He shrugged. "I suppose it's because I want to get out of my parents' house. And perhaps it's because I thought traveling with a cute kitsune would be fun."

Blushing, I folded my arms. "*Baka*! Don't get cocky. I don't like humans, and that is that."

"And yet you blush."

I raised a finger, and a blue flame appeared at the tip. "Do you want to survive this journey?"

He held up his hands. "I joke, I swear! I'll stop."

I extinguished the flame. "Good. I didn't want to have to come up with some story for Ichika-sama. It would have been a hassle."

"Well, I'm glad I didn't have to put you through that much trouble."

I rolled my eyes as we walked farther into the city.

Although I could view a lot of this city from the mountain, the area was still different from what I could ever have imagined. People occupied every street and walkway, no matter which way I looked. They didn't even seem to glance our way as we too walked on this strange, hard ground. I glanced down to find the ground gray and solid, as if made of rock. I never remembered there being rock like this in Kyoto. What was this substance? And why did no one else take note of it?

The buildings stood a lot more crowded than I remembered them. How could humans live like this? Sure they could go up where the shrine was for nature, but we were already five minutes outside the shrine, and I couldn't feel a connection to nature at all. My hands shook.

"Are you okay?" Yamato glanced over.

I nodded. "I'm fine."

I didn't like how he kept asking that. Why would a kid like him care? Although I suppose many who looked at us thought we were the same age. Little did they know that I was much, much older than anyone around us.

Looking up, I found strange strings that hung from

one pole to the other. They were dark and I could not make out what purpose they served. At first I thought they were supposed to hold lanterns, but that didn't seem to be the case.

I pointed up at them. "What are those?"

Yamato glanced up at what I was pointing at. "Those are electric wires. Never touch unless you want to see how strong your powers are."

"What do you mean?"

He shook his head. "Nothing. Just don't touch them."

What he said was confusing, but I decided not to ask any more about them. They were too ugly to wonder about any longer.

The most surprising thing was that yokai still occupied the area, yet no human seemed to respond to them. Yamato still looked down at his phone, as if purposefully ignoring them. Rumors stated that if some of these spirits realized you could see them, they would attach themselves. Or at least that was what some teens said to scare each other as they ventured up the shrine trail. I doubt many yokai wanted humans to see them. Maybe things were easier that way.

A little *kappa* wandered onto the sidewalk, screaming as people were almost stepping on him. Yamato sidestepped, so he didn't hurt him. I bent down and grabbed the kappa youngling and placed him on my shoulder for the time being until we were out of the crowd.

"Thank you!" the kappa's squeaky voice said in my ear.

"Don't mention it."

As we passed under a bridge and out the other side, I noticed a small pond.

"Here you go, little guy." I placed him down on the grass. "Go in the water where your friends are."

The kappa waved and hurried off to be with his friends. I turned back to Yamato, who was watching the kappa.

So he could see it. It was one thing to see a kitsune like me, who was powerful, but another to notice something that didn't possess much spiritual energy yet. If he bore this much spiritual power, it was no wonder Inari wanted me to help him on the right path, whatever that was. Much time has passed since any priest could see us yokai.

"You better hurry or we will miss the train out of here and have to wait a few hours for the next one."

My eyes widened as I hurried off after him. He was

right—we barely made the train as the doors closed the moment we stepped on, which scared me. It clearly wasn't yokai who closed them. How did they close like that? I turned to Yamato, wide-eyed.

He laughed. "You have much to learn about this world."

CHAPTER EIGHT

Late Summer 1542 (Muromachi Period)—Nagasaki

I tried to stay under the tree cover as the rain dumped down from the gray sky. My purple-and-black kimono clung to my skin. Everything I owned was wet—even the snacks I wanted to eat later. The rain had ruined them, all thanks to the fact we still found ourselves near the ocean during the late summer months. Sometimes the days would be perfect, but on a day like today, when a typhoon made its way across southern Japan, the rain never seemed to stop.

Glancing over at Akikumo, I found him sitting cross-legged with his eyes shut, his own white kimono soaked and stained from the mud and grass. He always liked to meditate during these conditions. I didn't quite understand why he chose to but I took a seat next to him and prayed that we would find somewhere to replenish my snack bag. He owed me more snacks, as he was the one who wanted to come back down here. We were supposed to be heading north already to go back to his home in the Hida Mountains, as we hadn't been to that region in quite a while.

We spent most of our time in the Kujuu Mountains this past century, as that was where his home was on the Kyushu Island. The area was pleasant in the winter, but I found the summers a lot hotter than I liked, and typhoons always came at the end of the season and they never seemed to end.

Currently we found ourselves traveling once again until Akikumo stopped and meditated like this. Then the rain came and soaked through everything I owned. He was a lot more patient than I, that was for sure.

I didn't argue, however, mainly because he threatened to not buy me snacks, and I really liked mochi, especially the sweet ones with fruit. If I stayed quiet and didn't bother him in this state, then the next town we traveled to he would buy me a couple. I couldn't wait.

Akikumo made me visit any human settlement he went into now, and I was getting used to them once again. I stayed near Akikumo, however, and didn't interact more than I needed. So far no incidences had occurred.

As I sat there across from Akikumo, I saw his ears twitch. Although his okami ears appeared similar to my kitsune ears, he always seemed to be able to hear farther than I could. I didn't know if it was because he meditated and listened or if the difference was something physical. He picked up noises over ten thousand steps, but I barely heard past fifty. Perhaps if I meditated like him, I one day would be able to do the same.

Closing my eyes, I decided to practice as well. I sought out anything that wasn't rain. I listened as the water hit the ground all around us and picked out the sounds as it hit the leaves on top of the trees. Wind roared through the branches, but all those things stood close to me. I wondered how far Akikumo could hear right now.

I peeked an eye open to find him still sitting there, his ears occasionally twitching. I wagged my two tails back and forth, which would distract him from what he was listening to.

"I know you are doing that on purpose, Ketsue-chan."

I stopped and tried not to giggle. He was so easy to get a response from. He never got mad at me either, as I saw his lips turn in a slight smile. I watched him some more since I was already bored with trying to listen. His hair was drenched and clung to his face and clothes. All I could hear was rain, and all I could smell was wet trees and dirt. I wondered when I could bug him again, or how long he would hold this for. As I was about to see how far I could move before he would say something, both his ears moved straight up and his eyes shot open.

"There was a landslide in Nagasaki. We must hurry and help them."

I shook my head. "You can't be serious. There won't be much we can do in this weather. And besides, it's the humans' fault for living in one place for a lengthy period of time. Don't they know one should travel with the season as the kami intended? That is why certain plants grow in regions during different times of the year. Even the animals understand that."

"Ketsueki…"

Rolling my eyes, I stood up. "Fine, but you know as well as I that I am right."

Akikumo said nothing as he led us down the mountainside and out of the forest. Nagasaki was a town right on the ocean that seemed to use a lot of ships. I still didn't understand why humans didn't listen to nature but always fought what they couldn't control. If they opened their eyes to the possibility that forces stronger than them existed and they should act accordingly, there would be fewer disasters. That is, if humans contained the capacity to work together. From what I noticed, such a thing was impossible.

The closer we got to the town, the stronger I smelled the unearthed ground. Akikumo was correct—there was a landslide. It amazed me he had picked up such a thing at that distance. If only I was as skilled as he was, then perhaps I could hear where aburaage was frying in the distance so I didn't have to wander all around trying to find it.

As we entered the town, we both transformed into our human form. Humans ran in every direction, afraid that the land would slide more or trying to help the people stuck in the building under all the debris. Akikumo acted fast in asking what people needed. He helped use tools to dig out some of the dirt that covered the doors to help the people out of their homes before the weight of the rock caved in their roof.

I hadn't seen such chaos since the day my mother and father died. This was different, however, as the disaster was not from a war but something natural. I wondered if life would have been different if I had lost my family in this way instead of during a battle. Would people have stopped to help me? Or would they have kept on walking by?

Shaking my head, I tried to push those memories away. This was neither the time nor the place. I needed to help these people, even though they didn't help me in my time of need. Akikumo would be disappointed if I didn't grow up and forgive them.

But if I was honest, I would never forgive them for the way they had treated me.

I just needed to act the part in order for Akikumo to let me stay with him. I wouldn't interact with humans without him near. And he would always be near, so it was fine.

"My son! My son is under there!" a woman screamed as she ran around. No one seemed to pay her much mind as they went to the primary areas that needed help. It reminded me of when I was begging for help from the humans who had ignored me.

I stepped up to her. "Where is your son?"

Tears ran down her face, although it was hard to tell from all the rain. Her soaked kimono was a dark pink rose color now stained with the dirt that slid off the hillside.

"He was playing behind the house! I had no idea!" She wailed further. I started to understand why no one stopped for her as I found it difficult for her to articulate what exactly she needed.

I grabbed her by the shoulders, even though I barely came up to her chin. "Where is he?"

She pointed over to the debris. "He is under there! I pray to the kami he is still alive! He has to be."

I listened closely, just like Akikumo taught me. I heard a child crying from underneath there. Examining the debris closer, I found that there was a small hole that I could enter with my fox form. Listening some more, I came to the conclusion that the kid was only a few years old and could fit through the hole as well. If he was smart, he would have climbed out already, but he was probably too scared to move.

Glancing around, I found that everyone else was on the other side of the landslide, trying to get to the buildings. If I transformed into a fox, only this woman would see. I was going to save her son. Would she get mad at me for being a yokai once she found out? There was no time to think about it—I must save the boy, otherwise I wouldn't be any better than these humans.

I transformed into my fox form, my fur matted from the heavy rain. Even more, the poor twin tails appeared less beautiful than normal. I darted into the hole and searched for the child. As I climbed through the debris, I found the child crying and not noticing I was there. I bit at his collar and dragged him out of the debris through the tunnel. He didn't fight it but seemed to calm down as he realized I was rescuing him.

As I dragged him from underneath the debris, I felt something hit me straight in the head. Letting the boy go, I jumped back to find the lady kicking me with her waraji. She grabbed her son and kept hitting me with her *waraji*.

"Yokai! *Yajuu*! Get away from my son!"

I knew I shouldn't, but I snapped at the old woman

and bit her foot. Blood filled my mouth, but I didn't lose control like I did when I was younger. I was angry that she would treat me like this after I had saved her son.

"It bit me! This yajuu bit me! Someone help me destroy this yokai! It is an abomination and will bring destruction."

Kuso, I was in trouble. Akikumo was going to scold me. I bolted toward the forest, away from the humans that gathered around me. They tried to chase after me, but I flew past them, even in this heavy rain.

I heard Akikumo calling for me in the distance, but I kept running. I shouldn't have transformed into a fox in front of the humans, but I wanted to help the boy. It wasn't fair that these humans labeled me as a yajuu even though I was helping them. As I found a modest cut-out in the hillside, I curled up into a ball and hid. It kept the rain off my wet fur, and I hoped the rain would soon pass so I once again would be dry.

Laying my head down, I wondered if Akikumo would give up looking for me and move on. I had let him down. He had told me to stay close to him in case anything happened. I failed as a yokai.

Half an hour passed as I sat there, curled up in a ball,

tears running down my snout. I heard a crunch of leaves under a warajii. Glancing up, I found Akikumo standing before me. I turned my head away from him.

He bent down. "It's all right. You were trying to help."

"I know that. And the *busu* still tried to kill me."

Akikumo let out a sigh as he transformed into a wolf and snuggled next to me. "Humans are fragile beings and have to put up a defense if they want to survive."

"They need to learn to trust."

"But have you learned to trust? Trust works both ways, my dear Ketsue-chan. Now, let us rest until the rain passes. Then we can head north away from this place."

I nodded and leaned my head against his fur. He was warm compared to the cool air. I closed my eyes and drifted off to sleep, vowing to never forgive humans ever again.

CHAPTER NINE

Present day—Train from Kyoto to Nagoya

My eyes were glued to the other side of the train window as we traveled past what humans called kilometers upon kilometers. Not only had Kyoto changed drastically, but so did the rest of Japan. I kept having to close my mouth as it dropped open, seeing the state of colonization of humans. How did they become so vast in only two centuries? Never had they increased this many in numbers before.

I noticed, however, that fewer yokai occupied the

space between towns, even though fewer humans still inhabited those areas. I pondered why that could be. Perhaps it was because so many humans now traveled around the country and could come across these yokai homes. Humans used to fear travel due to unfriendly yokai attacks and human bandits. Now, however, they no longer feared those things, one because they no longer saw the yokai and the other because more rules were enforced. I wasn't sure if either of those things were a good thing or a bad thing.

Yamato leaned his head on the glass, his eyes closed and his phone still in his hand. I didn't quite understand what use those devices possess, other than to distract one's attention with. I had seen many humans carry them as they venture up the mountain, pointing them at each other as the other person paused. Were they like cameras? And if so, how come humans never looked away from them?

"It's rude to stare," Yamato commented as he peeked an eye open.

I rolled my eyes. "I wasn't staring at you in particular. I simply find you humans to be peculiar."

He straightened up and put his phone away. "Oh, and why is that?"

I shrugged. "Well, for starters, you humans obsess over the strangest things, such as that square device of yours."

"My phone?"

"Yes. And there is all this expansion and settling in one place. You realize it is smarter to travel as nature intended, right?"

He laughed. "Easier said than done."

"It used to be, as long as you stayed in groups. Animals travel with the seasons, knowing where food was to be found and better weather. Instead, you humans stay put and don't listen to nature."

"It's because of agriculture. We planted crops and stayed in one spot."

I folded my arms. "That's stupid. Do you not realize that plants grow in certain seasons to help with illnesses and nutrition for that season? Such as the nettle that is high in minerals and vitamins during the spring months after you fast during the winter. Now humans hardly use the plant and it's everywhere."

"Humans grew and now find it impossible to move around. Besides, few people in the past traveled since it's so dangerous. It's not like the terrain is human friendly."

He made a valid point, and it surprised me he possessed knowledge of Japan's history. I let out a sigh. "Whatever, humans still make little sense."

He raised an eyebrow. "And yokai do?"

I glanced around, making sure no one heard him call me that. No one seemed to pay attention. "We make a lot more sense than you do. We don't complicate things and are connected with the kami and nature. We want something and we try to get it. Unlike your kind, we don't make up excuses."

"Then why have you waited so long to go searching for this Akikumo?"

"That's Akikumo-sama to a human like you."

"Sorry. Akikumo-sama. Isn't he an okami? Do they even exist any longer?"

I wanted to slap this punk but decided not to. I didn't need to explain to Ichika why his face was bruised when we got back. "There are a lot of things you humans don't understand, and there is no way that Aki-chan could have passed away without me knowing."

"Aki-chan? Was he your boyfriend or something?"

My face turned red. Why did Inari want me to take this back-talking kid? He was getting on my nerves more and more as each second passed. "Aki-chan was not my boyfriend. He was a mentor, best friend, and someone I could look up to. He taught me everything I know."

"So he taught you how to be a troublemaker?"

I let out another breath. "You are troublesome."

He shrugged. "I try. But I am wondering, how do you spell Akikumo. It's not exactly a common name."

"With the *kanji* for sun and moon, and the kanji for cloud. My name, Tsuki Ketsueki, is the kanji for moon and blood. He gave me the kanji for blood and took th kanji for moon from his name and gave it to me as a family name since he didn't have one."

"So he adopted you?"

"In a sense. Sometimes he told others I was his daughter, but I think that was so they wouldn't be confused as to why we traveled together. He didn't feel like a father to me, even when we first met."

"When was that?"

I was surprised by his interest in my past. It wasn't like I cared about his. "About seven hundred years ago."

"Wow. You're old."

I frowned and adjusted my white-and-blue floral kimono as he laughed. He grabbed some device and placed it on his ear, then pulled his phone back out and started playing on it again. I sighed as I looked back outside. How could this much have changed over only two centuries? I wished I were back to a much simpler time when I didn't need to keep up with these humans. It surprised me what they accomplished in such short lifespans, but I supposed it was because there were so many of them now.

What would happen to us yokai? Would we still find a place in this world, or would we have to move on to the netherworld?

We reached our first stop in Nagoya, and I followed Yamato as he led us toward the other train. It still smelled foul, so we weren't quite to the mountains yet. Apparently we couldn't get on one train and reach our destination. There were so many people that I reached out and grabbed Yamato's hand. He didn't seem to mind, as it kept us from getting separated. Once we neared our area, Yamato stopped.

"We have two hours before our train leaves. Do you want to grab lunch?"

I nodded. "Yes please. I only packed for the hiking trip but packed nothing for lunch while we traveled."

He led us toward an entire line of shops. I gasped, not believing so many stores existed in this area. They were all lit and decorated with many colors that I didn't even think were possible. Everything was so bright. I didn't quite know what to expect. There were even symbols I didn't understand. It was like a different type of writing. I concluded it was from the other continents that had influenced Japan over the years.

Most people wore the same things as Yamato, and I only saw a couple of people in yukatas. It was strange, as people used to wear kimonos all the time. Kimonos, I felt, were more practical and beautiful. At least we yokai wouldn't change what we wore.

"Well," he began. "What do you want to eat?"

I bit my lip. "Do any of these restaurants serve aburaage?"

Yamato laughed. "So that legend is true. All right, we can eat at the sushi bar."

He led us to one and we entered the restaurant. I gasped as plates of food moved from one side of the restaurant to the other.

"What sugure is this?" I exclaimed as Yamato pulled out a seat for me.

"Sh, someone will hear you. It's all electricity and

machines."

I took a seat and cocked my head to the side. "Electricity? Machines?"

"Yeah, you remember those black strings you saw?"

I nodded.

"Those carry power that we call electricity. It powers machines like this one."

"Do the machines possess souls?"

He shook his head and laughed. "No, nothing of the sort."

I was about to ask him more questions when I caught sight of my dearest aburaage moving in front of me. I snatched it before anyone else could and clapped my hands. Suddenly another moved by and I grabbed it as well. As I reached for the third, Yamato grabbed my wrist.

"How about you eat those and then get more? Don't worry, there is plenty."

He almost sounded like Akikumo. I couldn't help it, though, as much time had passed since I'd gotten to feast on my favorite food. Sure people left it out as offerings at the Inari shrine, but the more powerful kitsune got first dibs and there was hardly ever any left for me. If there was, it was old and appeared spoiled. I usually ate it anyway and immediately regretted it.

I clapped my hands together. "*Itadakimasu.*"

Yamato grabbed a couple of plates of sushi and clapped his hands together.

"Itadakimasu."

I took a bite and was instantly thankful for Yamato finding this place. They filled the aburaage with sesame rice, like an *inarizushi* typically was. Did humans eat like this constantly? There were many people in here, not to mention we came across many other places to eat. Did people not cook for themselves any longer? No wonder they had time to create all of this.

"What is it?" Yamato asked.

"It's surprising how much food there is with how many people are in this city. I wouldn't have thought it possible. You humans must have really figured out the whole agriculture thing."

"I suppose it would be strange. You weren't around when Japan expanded and started trading with other countries."

"I was around when they first came about."

"Now it's possible to be in another country in a matter of hours."

My eyes widened. "How is that possible?"

"You know those things you see moving in the sky?"

"Yes. One of the other kitsune said they were called planes and could hold people, but I didn't believe him."

"It's true. They hold people and you can travel the world."

I was both surprised and a little disappointed. Humans could travel anywhere? Why would they want to do that when there was plenty in Japan?

I frowned. "I don't want to go to any of those other countries. They don't worship our kami and try to bring different gods to this land."

He held back a laugh. "That wasn't something I expected you to say, but I suppose it makes sense."

"Aki-chan worked for the kami. I was there when the foreigners came. They look nothing like us."

"That is true. Well, maybe after we are done looking for your friend, I can show you some more of Japan and how it has changed."

I narrowed my eyes. "Why would you want to do that?"

He shrugged. "I suppose it's just fun watching you be so flabbergasted at everything. It is quite entertaining."

I frowned as I ate another inarizushi. "Well you won't have to worry because when I find Aki-chan, I will stay with him and we will get away from human cities like this." I glanced down at my dish. "Although I have to admit the food is good."

Yamato laughed as we went on with our meal. I took many other plates of aburaage with many different fillings. My favorite was the pickled sakura as it possessed the right amount of sweet and sour.

Too bad I was being truthful about never wanting to set foot in another city again. Taking a deep breath, I sighed and fiddled with my magatama. I would trade all the aburaage in the world to be at Akikumo's side once again.

CHAPTER TEN

October 1578 (Azuchi-Momoyama Period)—Izumo

"I have a surprise for you, Ketsue-chan." Akikumo grinned as he fiddled with his white-and-red sode, grabbing whatever item he had hidden.

I cocked my head to the side, wondering what he wanted to give me. It didn't smell like food. As he pulled out a small strip of paper, I read the kanji inscribed on it.

This was a ticket to the banquet of the gods in Izumo.

My mouth dropped. There was no way he would take

me this year, was there? I only possessed two of my tails—I wasn't a full-grown kitsune yet.

"I don't understand. They won't let someone as young and inexperienced as me in, would they?"

He nodded. "I got permission to bring you this year. If anyone asks, you are my familiar. They consider me a kami since I spread any messages they need to the humans. So I pulled some strings and got you invited."

I bowed. "Thank you very much! I will not let you down!"

He laughed. "Nothing you do would ever disappoint me, Ketsue-chan. Now, let us get to Izumo so we can find you a new kimono and we can freshen up in the hot spring."

"Yes! Let's!"

Izumo was only a few hours from where we were traveling. For the month of October, Akikumo normally left me in the apartment he stayed at and would disappear during the day and get back late at night, if he came back at all. This year I would attend with him and assist with any duties he needed to perform. I would do my hardest to make him proud.

The only problem was that I knew he wanted to go to the human part of the city to pick out a kimono and visit the *onsen*. Yokai onsens, or bathhouses, were always more enjoyable than human's as then I didn't need to figure out the new customs humans made. Yokai kept the same customs throughout time.

Also, humans performed lewd acts at many of the mixed bathhouses. Akikumo seemed to know which ones still acted as areas to take baths and which ones acted as brothels. Sometimes though, he was incorrect. In those incidences, he would cover my eyes and lead me away from the area.

This time, however, we found an onsen that wasn't indecent. I leaned back and enjoyed the warm water on this cool autumn day. The crisp air filled my lungs, sweet and earthy. This bath was outdoors, but we were fortunate that the clouds didn't pour rain on us. Many people occupied the area, but Akikumo and I were able to find space in a little outlet of the bath.

Akikumo closed his eyes. "A bath after a lengthy journey is one of life's greatest delights."

"I agree, although I prefer our kind's onsens more."

"Don't worry, during our time in Izumo, we will attend our kind's as well. I just wanted to use this one to clean ourselves off after our trip."

I sighed. I didn't find human onsens as cleansing as

yokai's, yet Akikumo always insisted on going to a human bath first if possible. I did not enjoy sharing water with humans.

After we soaked for a while, we put on our new, clean kimonos. Mine was a mix of pink and red with white floral designs. Since we were meeting with the kami, I was wearing many layers that would be a struggle to walk up the steps with, but I would not complain as it was an honor. Akikumo's kimono was plain white with yellow and blue layers underneath. His hakama, however, was designed with blue clouds. The hakama suited him and I was glad we found it.

Once we were ready, we started toward the shrine. Humans crowded the area, as they usually did in Izumo this time of year. People gathered to pray to the gods that now gathered at the shrine. By the looks of it, the faith in the kami was still strong. Akikumo had warned many towns of religions that might affect the faith, but so far everything seemed fine.

Walking through the torii gate, the magical wooden structure transported us yokai into another world. Instead of the human crowd that once stood before us, kami and their familiars now lined up to enter the great shrine of Okuninushi.

The shrine looked similar to the shrine the humans created but was on a much more massive scale. Enormous twisted rope hung above the entrance. *Usagi* familiars scurried around, dressed in simple kimonos and making sure they attended to each kami. A usagi stepped up to us.

"Would your familiar like us to prepare her for the banquet?"

I frowned. Was my outfit not good enough? This kimono was from one of the most expensive shops that we could find. Even I had worn nothing so expensive.

Akikumo chuckled. "She means your hair and makeup. If you are offering, we shall accept."

"Thank you. Follow me this way." The usagi turned and started hopping toward one of the other buildings. I turned to Akikumo, who motioned me to go.

"I will find you after you finish. You want to appear your best, don't you?"

I nodded. "Yes, Aki-chan."

I hurried off toward the usagi, hoping this wouldn't end disastrously.

After what seemed to be forever, I was ready for the banquet. They allowed me to stay in my kitsune form and I could show off my two silky tails. I took great pride in my fur as it took a lot of effort to keep the red and black hairs clean and beautiful. They did my makeup and hair in a human fashion, as the usagi explained that the Okuninushi likes to keep up to date with human culture. I found this to be strange but didn't argue. He was the leader of all kami, so who was I to question?

The usagi showed me my face in a mirror, and I didn't even recognize myself. I often would look at myself in a mirror since Akikumo carried a mirror, as the object was sacred and showed everything's true nature without distortion. So I made sure I always looked somewhat decent most of the time.

Leading me back to Akikumo, the usagi took me to the enormous banquet hall. Dozens upon dozens of kami sat at what was the largest wooden table I ever thought imaginable. Akikumo sat near the middle with his katana to his side, and I sat down next to him, careful not to wrinkle my kimono. I could smell the jasmine and sandalwood he used as a perfume.

Akikumo looked at my face and hair and held back a laugh.

"What? You are the one who said to go with the

usagi."

"I know, but it is strange seeing you with such heavy makeup. It looks good."

I turned to stare at the empty table before me. "I want to wash it off right now."

"Not yet. Besides, look around. All the goddesses and familiars are dressed up in the same fashion. You don't stand out, so don't worry about it. Besides, we have another couple of weeks of festivities, so you will dress up often."

"Ugh. Maybe I shouldn't have come."

"Nonsense. This will be a lot of fun. Besides, you will be a lot happier once this table is full of food and drink."

My ears perked up. "Food?"

"Yes. All your favorite foods will be here."

My tails wagged back and forth. "Even aburaage?"

"Of course. Inari-sama is here as well. They are down near the end of the table. I can introduce you if you want."

I shook my head. "No, I'm too shy. They use kitsune as their familiars, correct?"

"Yes. I would think you would want to meet more of your kind. There should be a few who are helping them this month."

"But those are adult kitsune. I stand out being so young. Perhaps another time."

"Perhaps. But you need to meet more people. I fear I have made you into someone who doesn't understand how to socialize, even though that is all I do."

"What I do isn't a reflection on you, Aki-chan. It is all me."

"That is where you are wrong, Ketsue-chan. I gave you the name Tsuki, did I not? You are an extension of me in that way and represent me no matter where you are. Just as I represent you. There will be a time when you understand, but for now we shall enjoy our time in Izumo."

I nodded and resented not being able to trust others. Of course, I was always with Akikumo—he was the only one who showed me compassion. Anytime I revealed myself to others, they didn't want me near them. As for other yokai, well, they were always using Akikumo. He always did what they asked, leaving more work for him. I didn't enjoy that part of our journeys.

A kami sat down next to me and I bowed. Her kimono was a mix of deep maroon and light turquoise with the outer layer having a print of mountains.

"Hello. I am Konohanasakuya-hime. I am the kami of Mount Fuji. Who are you?" she asked, her voice as gentle as a spring breeze.

Akikumo bowed. "Hello Konohanasakuya-hime. I am Akikumo and this here is Tsuki Ketsueki. She is my familiar."

Konohanasakuya-hime nodded a bow. "It is nice to meet you. You have such beautiful tails. I bet it is hard to keep them so beautiful while working for a kami. I commend you."

My cheeks turned red. "Thank you very much."

"She works hard in cleaning them. Sometimes we are even late to appointments because she is still brushing them." Akikumo chuckled.

I gave him a look. "That's not true!"

Konohanasakuya-hime laughed at our bickering. "You two are exceptional friends. Your relationship will last forever. Now, excuse me as I discuss something with my husband. Thank you for making me feel welcome."

I nodded. "You are most welcome."

The kami turned to her husband and started discussing something in private. As I was about to turn to Akikumo, I found him talking to the kami on his left.

I had met this kami before—his name was Ryūjin, the kami of the ocean. I decided not to butt in and examined the room we were in some more. The shoji was simple and let in the outside light. As for the fusuma, a painting that seemed to depict the Kuniumi covered one side. The image was spectacular as Izanagi and Izanami reached down from the heavens and used the spear ame-no-nuboko to stir the oceans and create the first island, Onogoroshima. Rumors said that Akikumo was born when the first of Japan was created. Was this it? And if so, did that make him older than many of these gods?

As I pondered this, the shoji slid open and a tall man with braided black hair that had been woven into an intricate design stepped in. His long kimono wrapped to the floor, shining gold. Two of the usagi entered with him and bowed. All the kami around bowed, and I followed suit.

"Welcome, everyone! I thank you for traveling all the way here every year. The feast shall begin shortly. If you have any questions, please ask one of my familiars. Now. Let us enjoy this time of year once more!"

Everyone clapped in rhythm and I tried to follow along, but I didn't quite get the rhythm before the sound stopped. Akikumo held back a laugh.

Suddenly a flood of usagi came into the room and brought in plates upon plates of food. I drooled as they set some aburaage in front of me.

Maybe wearing all this makeup was worth it.

CHAPTER ELEVEN

Present day—Hida Mountains

I stretched and took in the fresh air. It smelled sweet and grassy. We had gotten away from all the miasma and human filth and were back in nature.

Two hours had passed since we started up into the forest from the last train station. From here on out, I didn't need to worry about the miasma or humans finding out what I was or messing something up. We finally found ourselves in the Hida Mountains.

Now I needed to figure out where Akikumo's home

was.

He owned so many homes that I couldn't quite remember where each one was. I also had a problem of paying attention to my surroundings, or at least that's what Akikumo used to say. There was also the fact that Japan had changed immensely since the last time I was here. The country even changed since Akikumo dropped me off in Kyoto.

Glancing back at Yamato, it surprised me he could keep up with me, especially with that large backpack. I had seen many of his type not being able to climb up to the top of the Inari shrine, let alone go on this backpacking journey in search for something that could be anywhere on this mountain. We told his parents we were on a pilgrimage through these mountains, and they didn't even question such a trip. Would he really do such a thing? I supposed if he could keep up with me this far; I had underestimated him.

Taking in another deep breath, I smelled the fresh leaves of the beech and oak. On the lower levels of the mountain, I felt immersed in the thick foliage, but the higher we got, the more dispersed everything became. I preferred the thick forest compared to the mountaintop as the air felt much warmer, but Akikumo always insisted on having his home near the top of the mountain. He said the view of Japan was most beautiful, not to mention that way he was closer to the stars and our ancestors.

Luckily we were traveling during the summer so we didn't have to worry about snow where we needed to go, although some places in this area possessed snow all year around. Akikumo used to love the snow. I didn't care for the stuff, but in my fox form I wasn't too miserable. I preferred summer beaches for sure.

"Do you have any idea where his home is?" Yamato asked as we ascended farther up the mountain.

I shook my head. "I just remember it was on this side of Mount Ikenodaira. There will be yokai we can ask and get an idea where to start."

"And where are these yokai?"

"At a hot spring at the edge of the forest... somewhere."

He stopped and stared at me. "You don't know, do you?"

"I know the general area. Cut me some slack—it has been a while. Inari gave us a map, correct?"

Yamato nodded as he pulled out the paper. "Yeah, I have it right here."

"Can you read it?"

He rolled his eyes. "Are you telling me you don't know how to read a map?"

"Maps are a human invention. I always wandered around."

"No, you followed Akikumo-sama wherever you went and didn't pay attention, didn't you?"

I frowned. "That's none of your business. Can you tell us where we are?"

"Yes. For your information, I learned how to read a map when I was very young."

"And here I assumed you were just a delinquent."

"By looks only. I am actually in the top of my class."

That information surprised me. According to some of the other kitsune and what I overheard the kids I had scared talk about, they all stayed in a building all day to learn about the world and how to speak. This somehow was a competition, and the top of the class meant you were the smartest and the winner.

"What? Are you surprised?" Yamato asked as he unfolded the map.

"I never expected someone like you, winning at school."

"Win at school? Never mind. It says here we need to

keep heading west and then north a bit and we will find it."

I stepped next to him and looked down at the paper he held. "How can you tell?"

"Because I've been keeping track on where we have been going with my phone. Not only that, but I also have a compass and an excellent sense of direction, unlike someone."

I turned and found that I was standing centimeters from him. We both looked at each other for a minute, and then I frowned.

"What's that supposed to mean?"

He shrugged. "Nothing. It just seems like you are constantly lost."

My cheeks turned red. "I will have you know I am a marvelous tracker and hunter! Akikumo taught me all I needed to survive!"

"Well, the world has changed since then. You are trapped in the old ways and need a 101 class on the present."

"A one-oh-one?"

"Forget it."

I put my hands on my hips and glared at him. "You humans assume you are so smart. You do not understand all the stuff I have seen. I have been alive for hundreds of years and I—"

Something dripped onto the top of my head. From what I remembered, I hadn't noticed clouds above us. I watched Yamato flinch as if something fell on him as well. Both of us looked up and saw a giant grotesque head. His eyes bulged out of his skull and looked down at both Yamato and me. Drool dripped down from its mouth as he kept his mouth open, ready to feast on his prey.

"*Tsurube-otoshi*! Run!"

I shoved Yamato forward to get him to start running as he was flabbergasted by the monster. The moment we moved, the creature pounced down on the ground, hopping after us. I shuddered at the sight of him. Akikumo and I ran into them twice before while traveling. While they were pretty weak for a yokai, I still wanted to make sure Yamato ran far enough away before I tried attacking him. Just in case.

Because the last time, Akikumo had saved me.

Branches of the beech and oak snagged at my yukata, which frustrated me as this was one of my favorite yukata that I wanted to show off to Akikumo. It was all this tsurube-otoshi's fault.

When Akikumo and I traveled, most beasts stayed away and never bothered us due to Akikumo's power radiating off him. I figured I possessed enough power to scare these beasts away, but apparently I was wrong. Which meant we would face a lot of creatures in these mountains. I was not looking forward to that.

Yamato still ran ahead of me, and I didn't suspect we would gain any more distance from the tsurube-otoshi. Transforming into my kitsune form, I relished in having my ears and tails back. But more importantly, now I could use my kitsunebi power and fight with my claws if need be.

Spinning around on my heels, I faced the creature. He still bobbed up and down after us as if all he cared about was eating some human flesh. He must not have realized I was a yokai. His hair flopped back and forth, and I could tell a while had passed since he had bathed as he reeked of sweat and rotting flesh.

I created a large flame in my hand. "Eat this, you worthless yokai!"

I threw the flame straight as his face. The creature screamed but kept charging forward. I did not want to use too much power on him in case bigger creatures were waiting in the dense forest. There were. I could sense them.

But I had no choice. The tsurube-otoshi still wanted to taste Yamato's flesh. I created another blue flame, focusing on my *ki* to make it exactly how I wanted it, and hurled the kitsunebi straight into the creature's eyes. He let out an ear-piercing scream and stopped coming toward us. He shook his head, but the flames would not go out. Jumping away, he hurried off back into the forest, the opposite direction from where we ran.

I let out a sigh when a twig snapped behind me. I raised my hand and created another ball of fire, ready to attack.

"Whoa! It's just me!" Yamato held up his hands, as if that would stop the pain of the kitsunebi.

I extinguished the blue flame and let out a sigh. "Don't scare me like that. Why weren't you still running?"

"And leave a damsel in distress behind? As if."

I shot him a look. "I am not a damsel in distress. I'm a lot more powerful than any of you humans could even dream."

Yamato tightened his hoodie around his waist and adjusted his backpack. "So you keep saying. Anyway, do you expect that creature will come back?"

I shrugged. "Probably not. Those flames hurt a lot. He will stay away if he knows what's good for him."

I looked down at my hands to find my nails long and clawlike. Right, I still appeared in my kitsune form. I realized, in that instant, Yamato didn't fear how I looked. No human had ever accepted me like this. Glancing back at him, he didn't seem fazed one bit. It was quite peculiar. However, I needed to transform back into a human. Letting my ears and tail disappear, I fixed my yukata.

Yamato gave me a surprised look. "Why don't you stay in your kitsune form in case the creature comes back?"

Finishing up with my kimono and checking to make sure my magatama hadn't fallen, I explained, "We are still likely to run into humans here. I can't get spotted in that form, or someone might cause trouble."

He raised his eyebrow. "You do it all the time at the shrine."

I let out a little laugh. "That's different. They are teens and it's at night. No one believes them anyway. Out here, people are looking for creatures like me, and if I give them proof, then I might not find Akikumo with all the chaos that would ensue. So I'll stay in human form."

"I guess that makes sense." He put his hands in his jean pockets, moving part of his hoodie that he tied around his waist out of the way. "Thanks. For saving me."

I studied him for a moment, surprised he would thank me like that. "Don't mention it. Besides, we will probably come across more problems, so don't get too comfortable. We aren't in the clear yet."

He laughed, but we both realized I was right—more creatures were waiting in this forest, and it was only a matter of time before they noticed we had entered their domain. And not only that, a human could see them.

CHAPTER TWELVE

Summer 1587 (Azuchi-Momoyama Period)—Hida Mountains

"Someone help me!" I screamed as I dashed through the forest, weaving between trees, trying to lose the yokai that followed me. From what I remembered, Akikumo called the enormous head a tsurube-otoshi. Whatever he was, he possessed the ugliest features I had ever laid eyes on. Bulged eyes, tangled hair, a stench that assaulted my nose. I wanted to get away from him, as I did not understand what he wanted from me.

The creature didn't seem to speak Japanese or at least any Japanese that I understood. He spoke with strange sounds and bounced after me in these dense woods.

Where was Akikumo? And why hadn't he come to my rescue?

"Help me! Aki-chan!" I yelled out into the woods, my mouth and throat dry as I had been running for a long while. Sweat was dripping down my hair and into my eyes, but I kept on going. Akikumo had told me to stay put while he checked on something ahead. After he disappeared for a few minutes, this thing came barreling down from a tree branch and started chasing me.

Tears flew off my face as I galloped faster and faster. Somehow this giant head kept up with me. I didn't understand how it was possible, but every time I looked back, he still trailed behind.

"Aki-chan!"

Suddenly a figure jumped out from behind a group of trees. I looked up to find Akikumo staring at the yokai. I hid behind him as he pulled out his katana and attacked the yokai, slashing his face. The creature yelped and tried to bounce away. Akikumo didn't let him, though, and ran after, attacking again and again. Blood poured onto the ground, splattering red over the tree foliage. Soon the tsurube-otoshi lay motionless on the ground, a pool of blood forming around him and soaking the grass and leaves.

Akikumo wiped away the blood that dripped down his face with his tenugi. His kimono was now stained with blood, the red almost appearing like it was a pattern contrasting the yellow cloth. "Come, Ketsue-chan. Help me dig a proper grave for this yokai."

"But he attacked us. He doesn't deserve a proper burial."

He shook his head. "No, everything deserves a proper burial, even our enemies. That way their spirit may rest."

I tried to understand but didn't quite get it. Why would one care so much about our enemies? Would they do the same for me if they had killed me? I doubted it, and yet Akikumo always seemed to put others first. I doubted any other yokai or human did the same. Was it because he was so old, or was this simply his nature?

As I helped dig a hole for the wretched creature that tried to attack me, I asked Akikumo a question that had occupied my mind for quite some time now. "Aki-chan, what were you like when you were young?"

He laughed as he tossed some dirt to the side. "What made you want to ask that question?"

"You are always so kind. Were you always like this, or did you learn it over time?"

He seemed to ponder this question for a bit before answering. "My purpose has always been to lead others, protect them, and send messages to and from the gods. If I did not do everything out of kindness and did not respect every living thing, then what would have been the point of it all?"

I frowned. That wasn't the answer I assumed he would give. I expected him to be like me and be a bit of a troublemaker, or at least a little freer. "What about as a child? Did you still possess all these responsibilities as a kid?"

Akikumo shook his head. "I was never a kid like you. I just have always been."

"You were never a kid? How is that possible?"

"During the beginning of time, many of the kami came into existence by fate. Some were born, but some were created. I was created."

I pursed my lips. "But you aren't like the other kami

since you don't have a shrine or worshippers."

"I suppose not, but I am thanked by many humans and kami, and that is its own praise."

He was too kind for his own good. If I possessed the power he did and worked nonstop through my entire life, I would want a little more praise. I doubt I could do it for the sake of life.

But I wasn't a kami like him.

Akikumo was on the border of kami and yokai. As he was still a wolf yokai, an okami, but he was much more powerful than that. He seemed similar to the kitsune who possessed nine tails and had lived for over a thousand years, becoming a kami themselves. I had met none of those kitsune, so I had no idea how strong they were or what they were like, but if they were anything like Akikumo, they must have been kind, benevolent creatures as well. How else would they achieve the status of kami without kindness?

We finished up creating a grave for the yokai and buried him. Akikumo clapped his hands together and bowed, as if thanking the kami for defeating the creature that attacked me. I mimicked him but didn't quite understand what I was supposed to pray about. After Akikumo finished up, he turned to me.

"Now, Ketsue-chan, I want to teach you a few tricks in case you get attacked again."

I tilted my head to the side, my red and black hair falling down to the side. "Like fighting with my teeth? I'm not as large as you, and I fear that I won't be able to bite hard enough before they hurt me."

"We will get to fighting techniques soon, but no, that isn't what I wanted to teach you. What I wanted to teach you is how to use your kitsunebi."

My eyes widened. "My kitsunebi? You think I am finally old enough?"

He nodded. "Yes. You are about the right age to harness that power. Although I am not a kitsune, I believe I can help you learn it."

I jumped up and down. Akikumo laughed as he led us higher up the mountain. I assumed he wanted to get away from the thick foliage so I wouldn't start a fire. I didn't blame him, as that was very possible. He also wasn't a kitsune and couldn't counter any of my kitsunebi.

The walk took another two hours, but we had reached where the trees were sparse. Even though we had traveled a considerable distance, I still possessed all my energy and jumped up and down, ready to train.

Akikumo sat on a large rock, taking in a few deep breaths.

"Are you going to teach me now?" My tails wagged back and forth as I punched my hands forward like I was fighting.

"Patience, Ketsue-chan. Remember, I am quite old and need to take a break."

I rolled my eyes. "Since when? You always are up and about. Being old has never stopped you before."

He ruffled the top of my head. "Oh, Ketsue-chan. Never change."

I wasn't sure what he meant by that but didn't give it much thought as he stood up and clapped his hands together. "Well then, shall I teach you the art of kitsunebi?"

"Yes please!"

"Then first we shall meditate."

I lowered my head in defeat. I wasn't getting anywhere with him. "Ugh…"

"I know you hate meditating, but you need to focus your mind before controlling the flame."

He sat back down but this time on the ground cross-legged. I followed suit as I learned I wouldn't be able to talk him out of it. If I do this, then I would have my kitsunebi.

"Close your eyes and search around within yourself. See what you feel."

I closed my eyes and tried to focus on myself. I felt… hungry. And tired now that I had to do this instead of getting to play with flames straightaway.

"Try to understand the energy that comes within. Do you sense your ki?"

I focused on the ki inside me. Akikumo had me do this a few times before and I was beginning to understand what he meant by it.

"I do."

"Now I want you to focus on that ki and will it into being. Your kitsunebi is part of you. It is part of your ki. If you can control your ki, you can control your flame."

I focused on my ki. If my kitsunebi was connected to the ki, I had to focus and understand myself. It was a hard concept, as there was much that one did not see but must feel to understand. Most who didn't see something with their eyes did not trust it or didn't believe it was real. As I had spent most of my life dealing with things that most did not see or comprehend, I kept an open mind. And I trusted Akikumo wouldn't lie to me. If he said ki was real, then it was.

We meditated for what seemed like hours, focusing on our ki and defining it and understanding how ki felt, how it moved, and how to call upon it when one needed. The only problem was, I still hadn't gotten to play with the fire yet.

I sighed. "Aki-chan, when will I get to make the kitsunebi?"

"I suppose you have worked hard today and deserve to make at least one flame. Fine, I shall tell you."

My tails wagged back and forth as I waited for him to explain.

"Now, what you need to do is will your ki to your hand and force it to become the fire. This takes a lot of concentration, so don't be frustrated if you don't get it on your first try."

I would get it on my first try—I had to. Such a feat would impress Akikumo and he would pat me on the head like he does when I do something outstanding. I loved it when he did that and tried my best at everything so I would get that reward.

Closing my eyes, I focused my best on trying to will my ki to my hand. The ki moved from my stomach to my chest and up my arm to my hand. I peeked open an eye and found no kitsunebi.

"It didn't work!"

Akikumo chuckled. "You are so fun to watch. As I said, it takes some time before you can master kitsunebi. Don't worry though, as we will keep working on it until you are the best of all the kitsune."

He patted my head, making me blush a little. I had failed, yet he still rewarded me. I was thankful for such a great mentor.

CHAPTER THIRTEEN

Present day—Hida Mountains

Yamato kept looking at his phone. I presumed he was figuring out where we were on the map as he held the paper open, leading us to where Inari pinpointed.

I would admit, I felt pathetic not being able to figure out where we needed to go. What if Inari hadn't made me take Yamato with me? What if they had let me go on my own? Would I have been able to find my way through this forest? Or would I haven't even been able to get to here as I didn't know how to use the trains and felt sick from all the miasma?

Inari knew I wouldn't have been able to do this by myself. They not only wanted me to help Yamato learn more of our world but also knew he would be better at directions. I was thankful for that, as they were smart in how they paired us together. I would need to thank them when this came to an end, one way or another.

I didn't want to go back even though Inari was nice enough to put this together for me. I didn't fit in with the rest of the kitsune and was always fighting with Ichika. I was a free spirit that was meant to roam like Akikumo—I wasn't meant to serve a shrine.

Yamato stopped and I ran straight into him, falling back on my butt. I blushed as he turned and held out his hand.

"Sorry, I didn't mean to stop so abruptly."

I grabbed his hand and he helped me up. He held my hand a little longer than I wanted, and I pulled it back. His skin was warm, and I realized it had been a while since I touched anyone's skin. Akikumo and I used to be close and hug and snuggle on frigid nights, but after being at the shrine, no one wanted anything to do with me.

How did I never realize that?

"Why did you stop?" I asked, pushing back the thoughts of my own loneliness.

"Oh, I was going to say we are coming up to a fork in the path. One way is shorter, but according to the map, Inari-sama wants us to take the longer path."

I furrowed my eyebrows. "Did they say why?"

He shook his head. "No."

Looking over the strange markings, I shrugged. "Maybe they didn't see the other path. Going the shorter route makes sense, doesn't it?"

"Yeah, I suppose so. Other than it being a little steeper, it doesn't appear to be any different."

"Well then, lead the way."

"Since you can't read the map?"

I gave him a look and shoved him forward. "Baka! Just go."

His shirt was soft and warm. I looked down at my hand after I removed it. How long had it been? Why was this so strange to me?

We trekked up the hill. Yamato wasn't kidding when he said it was steeper. I needed to walk around more as I noticed my body felt sore. When I was with Akikumo, I was the fittest I had ever been. Even though the Inari shrine was on a hill, I hadn't been moving around enough.

We came upon a small clearing with large rocks that I could rest on. I hoped Yamato came to the same conclusion as I didn't want to appear weak.

"I think we should rest." Yamato folded up the map and put it in his pocket. "We should get to our destination before the sun sets."

I nodded. "Yeah, it is probably a good idea for a human like you to rest. You don't want to overdo it on the first day."

He rolled his eyes as he drank some water. I jumped up on a rock and sat down. I smiled as I looked up at the sky. A long time had passed since I got to enjoy the wilderness like this.

"I'm still surprised Inari-sama didn't indicate to use this path. The route saves us over an hour."

I shrugged. "Again, they probably overlooked it."

"A kami overlook something? Aren't they supposed to be all knowing?"

I bit my lip. He made a valid point. Why didn't Inari mark the path that was shortest? Perhaps they knew something that we didn't.

Well, it was too late to worry about it now. I would simply stay alert.

"I wouldn't think about it too much. It's too late to go back now."

Yamato nodded. "Yeah, I suppose you are right. Well, do any of the woods we have been in seem familiar to you?"

I glanced around. "Kind of? But trees grow, trees fall, fires come… The forest is always changing even without humans. Even in the different seasons, the forest can appear different."

Yamato took in the scenery. "I suppose you are right." He took a deep breath and closed his eyes. I watched him closely, curious what a human like him was doing. He acted like Akikumo when he was in the wilderness and taking in everything. A human couldn't sit still long enough to appreciate life and everything in it, could they? I hadn't seen it often, yet this kid who the priest believed brought shame on their family name seemed a lot calmer in nature than he ever had at the shrine.

Maybe Inari was wrong—maybe Yamato didn't belong at the shrine but belonged out in the wild like this. Just like I did.

I shook my head. No, that was impossible. Humans hated the wild. They wanted to control nature and destroy it. They didn't understand the beauty and power that came with the wilderness.

He opened his eyes, and I turned but knew he noticed that I was staring. "What is it?"

I shrugged. "Nothing. You are a lot different from what I assumed."

"And you are exactly how I imagined you would be."

I frowned. "What is that supposed to mean?"

"You are a troublemaker and don't budge for anything. You have your own way you look at life, and nothing will change that."

I stood up on my rock and folded my arms. "I will have you know that the reason I don't budge is because I have trained a long time to achieve this greatness."

He rolled his eyes. "Yeah. Sure."

"Hey! A lowly human like you would never—"

I stopped and noticed a thick miasma rolled into the area. This was not good.

"Kuso…," I whispered.

"What is that?" Yamato asked as he stood up on the rock to get away from the black substance.

"Miasma. And a very thick kind."

"What sort of yokai creates that?"

"The bad kind. Or a fallen god."

"Great."

I smirked at his sarcasm. I wonder if Akikumo felt similar to how I did when he'd first started training me. But it was not the time to ponder such things. I would need to act fast if I wanted to stop whatever yokai was going to attack.

Transforming into my kitsune form, I created a kitsunebi to have at the ready. I listened closely, my ears noting anything that seemed out of the ordinary. It appeared as if there were things slithering under the thick miasma.

"Do you see that?" Yamato pointed down at the black substance.

I nodded. "Yup. Stay away from it—it can't be good."

"That was the plan."

I scanned for any way out but found none. We would either have to wait for this to pass and hope it didn't notice us up on the rocks or wait for the yokai to attack so I could locate it and destroy it once and for all.

There was one thing I could do, although I knew such an action would weaken me, and if we came across more evil yokai, I might not be strong enough to defeat them. Then again, we needed to survive this either way.

I formed dozens of flames and scattered them straight into the miasma, hoping that I could locate the source.

Whatever it was seemed to slither around but didn't make a sound. Finally, after throwing another kitsunebi, it let out a wrenching scream.

A direct hit, but this fight was far from over.

The creature stood up and I gasped. She was a *harionago*. Hundreds of strands of hair slithered off the head of the harionago, ready to strike and hook whatever stood in her way. All those things we saw were her hair. I didn't even want to think about what would happen if one of those pierced Yamato.

Cackling, she painted a distorted finger at me. "Little kitsune, do you think you can survive my thorn hair?"

I shrugged. "I suppose I will have to in order to get away, now won't I?"

She cackled again. "Well, perhaps you might get away, but your human friend will not!"

She disappeared in the miasma again, and I looked all around, trying to figure out where she would attack first. I took a deep breath and listened attentively.

The harionago was going straight for Yamato.

I leaped over to the rock he stood on, and as I landed, I saw one of her thornlike hair strands strike at him. I pulled him out of the way so it wouldn't go through his heart like it intended, but it still caught him in the arm.

Yamato screamed in pain, but at least the pain was a lot less than if it went through his chest. I formed another kitsunebi and threw it down at the miasma.

"You won't be able to find me!" The yokai cackled. "You won't stop me!"

At that point, I knew she was right. I couldn't tell where she was. A thornlike strand wrapped around Yamato's ankle and pulled him down. I grabbed his arm and tugged him back on the rock.

But the creature was too strong. I had to do something.

There was another attack I could do with my flames but always preferred not to as I had once almost burned down an entire forest out of fear of it going out of control. She left me with no choice, however, and I had to use it.

Calling upon all my ki, I created a flame that would ignite the entire area that was full of miasma. I took a deep breath and let the fire burn everything it touched.

The creature wailed, crying to make the burning stop. I watched as she ran back and forth, her hair lashing out each way, but it could not hit us with the flames engulfing everything in its path. I pulled Yamato back up and kept him away from the fire.

The harionago's wailing stopped, and all I could hear was the crackling of the fire as it burned up the leaves and bushes that surrounded us. Soon the miasma disappeared, and all that was left was the blue flame.

Now for the hard part.

Taking in a deep breath, I willed the fire to come back to me. It was a part of me—an extension. I couldn't let the flames get out of control or else they would destroy this entire forest. I was strong enough to do it—I was strong enough to will the fire back into me.

One more breath in and out, smelling the stench of burnt flesh and hair, I was able to slowly bring the fire back into myself. Soon all the flame was gone, and I collapsed down on the rock.

I did it—I maintained complete control over my kitsunebi.

CHAPTER FOURTEEN

October 1590 (Azuchi-Momoyama Period)—Odawara

The gentle leaves began to fall, painting the forest a beautiful hue of orange and red. The air was crisp and smelled of fallen leaves and soaked earth. The color of nature matched my fur, and I turned into a full animal to disappear in a pile of leaves. Akikumo laughed as I stuck my head out.

"I bet you can't see me!"

"Even if I might not see you, I most definitely can hear you."

I jumped out of the leaves and frowned. "What's that supposed to mean?"

He bent down and rubbed the top of my head. "That you are a typhoon in a kitsune's body."

I ran back into the pile of leaves. "Yeah, well, you won't be able to find me if I stay quiet!"

"Is that a challenge?" Akikumo asked as he transformed into his wolf form.

I didn't answer but kept running into the woods. I would need to be quiet if I wanted to lose him and prove that I too could be an exceptional hunter.

So far I hadn't won, but today would definitely be my day.

I was smaller than Akikumo, so I had that going for me. I darted through the bushes, hoping Akikumo couldn't follow.

Knowing him, though, he would find a way.

I heard rabbits and birds running in opposite directions, hoping I wasn't after them. Although I was peckish, I didn't feel like hunting. No, I wanted to prove once and for all that I could win a game against Akikumo. If I could beat a kami, then I was unstoppable.

I zigzagged around, keeping an ear out for Akikumo.

Thus far I hadn't heard any sound coming from him, but unlike him, I didn't possess acute hearing. I would have to increase the distance between the two of us in order to really hide.

A few minutes passed, and I felt that I had run enough. I jumped into a pile of leaves under a tree and made sure all my fur was covered. I waited a bit, listening to see if Akikumo at least figured out the area I had hidden. If I was lucky, it would take him a while.

But I was never that lucky.

It wasn't long before Akikumo came walking into the area, his yellow eyes scanning all around. I stayed quiet and tried to control my breathing even though I was out of breath from running so long.

"I wonder where Ketsue-chan could be… I guess she isn't in this area. I should probably head back."

I snickered a little and watched as the white wolf before me turned back around and leaped at the pile of leaves I was hiding in.

"Gotcha!"

We laughed as we tumbled around the forest floor, leaves messing up both our fur. I couldn't stop giggling as Akikumo flung leaves on top of me.

"Fine! You win!" I tried to knock the leaves off of

me, but Akikumo kept grabbing a bite with his mouth and flinging them in my direction.

"I have no idea what you mean. I don't see you—you blend in too much with the surrounding. It's as if you are invisible!"

"Stop it! You are messing up my fur!"

A snap of a twig made both of us stop and turn to find a giant black wolf watching us intently with its blue eyes. I hid behind Akikumo, yipping.

Akikumo transformed into his okami form. "*Otouto?*"

Otouto? Was Akikumo saying this was his younger brother? I didn't know that Akikumo had a brother, unless he was just saying this wolf was his brother because they were of the same species.

The black wolf transformed into a large okami. He had much broader shoulders than Akikumo and looked like a warrior. His hair was as black as the night sky and his eyes almost appeared like stars. He wore a red *hitatare* with a black sheathed katana wrapped with red leather at his side, indicating he was a *samurai*. I wondered if he had battled in any wars or if he was like Akikumo and had it for his work.

"*Ani!*" The man approached Akikumo and wrapped

his arms around Akikumo.

Akikumo grinned from ear to ear. "It has been a long time!"

"You are telling me! And here I find you in the middle of the forest, playing with some kitsune. I thought you were a strict, no-fun okami."

Akikumo gestured for me to come forward. "This is Tsuki Ketsueki. Ketsue-chan, this is my otouto Yamiyo. I don't think I've seen him in, what, a few centuries now?"

Yamiyo slapped Akikumo's back, causing Akikumo to jump a little. "And then some! You are too work-oriented, ani. But I see that you adopted a daughter. This is an enormous surprise."

"She isn't my daughter. She is more like a mentee."

"But you gave her a kanji of your name, did you not? You are closer to her than a mentor."

I transformed into my kitsune form and bowed. "It is an honor to meet you, Yamiyo-sama."

He let out a roar of a laugh. "Please, call me Yami-chan. I don't care for formalities. At least not with yokai."

I bowed again. "Thank you very much, Yami-chan."

Yamiyo turned back to Akikumo. "I am very

surprised you are taking care of this kitsune though. I thought you swore to always wander alone, as you must keep your mind on work and work only."

Akikumo blushed. "Perhaps I got lonely."

"Well if you were so lonely, why didn't you come find me so we could have a drink? You know I will always keep you company."

"You have been busy with countless wars. I figured you didn't have time for little ol' me."

"Nonsense! Now, I am heading to Odawara to help finish taking over the town and strengthening the stronghold. Will you join me there for at least one round of sake?"

Akikumo rolled his eyes. "One you say? More like a dozen."

Yamiyo let out a roar of a laugh. "You know me too well, ani!"

I followed the two men as Yamiyo led us to the town. This was not something I ever expected, but seeing Akikumo relax a bit with another okami made me smile. He deserved to relax after all the work he had done over the centuries. Maybe this could be that day.

The area still smelled of war.

I smelled blood and smoke as we entered the town. I wrinkled my nose as I glanced at Akikumo. He patted my back, letting me know he understood my dislike of the area, but said nothing. I supposed we couldn't turn back now that we were with his brother. I simply hated entering cities that still smelled of human battles as it reminded me of the horrors of my home.

We all had transformed into our human forms before entering the city. Apparently the humans that Yamiyo battled with had no idea of his true identity. He had battled in many, many wars, which I did not understand. Why would a yokai similar to Akikumo want to battle with humans?

Yamiyo led us to a small shop, and we sat on our knees at the table.

"Sake! And bring at least three bottles to start!" he ordered the hostess, who wore a simple pink kimono and apron. She nodded and went into the back to retrieve the sake. Moments later she came back with three narrow clay pitchers and three cups. She set them down before us and left us to enjoy the sake alone.

I glanced at Akikumo, who had never let me partake in sake before. I wanted to try it though, so I gave him the widest, saddest eyes I could.

He let out a breath. "Fine. But just this once and no more than two glasses."

I smiled at Yamiyo, who laughed. "You are wrapped around this girl's finger, aren't you?"

Akikumo poured sake into each of our cups. "Oh, you have no idea what I put up with. You know how much aburaage I have had to buy for her? It is ridiculous."

I pouted. "But it's the best."

"Yes, and the most expensive."

"What do I care? I don't pay for it."

Yamiyo let out a roar of a laugh. "I can see why you keep her around, ani. She is quite a rascal."

Akikumo held up his glass. "To fate and order!"

Yamiyo held up his glass as well. "To family and friends!"

"*Kanpai!*" they both said and downed their drinks. I took a sip of my own and my eyes widened. It was sour but sweet at the same time. It had almost a bite on the aftertaste. Never had I tasted anything like it.

"What do you think, Ketsue-chan?" Yamiyo asked. "Is it everything you had ever dreamed of?"

I nodded. "It is wonderful! This shouldn't be served to humans but to the gods instead."

Yamiyo shook his head. "I can't believe you haven't let her drink the sake of the gods and yokai. It is much better, and you know it."

Akikumo shrugged. "I didn't want to be a terrible influence. She still only has just received her third tail."

I smiled, proud of gaining my third tail. I was already three hundred years old now. I was about a third of the way to becoming as powerful as Akikumo. The time had flown by and I assumed so would the rest of the centuries, especially with Akikumo at my side. Between the two of us, we were unstoppable.

"So tell me, otouto, what have you been up to?"

Yamiyo downed another cup of sake. "Well, under the command of Toyotomi Hideyoshi, we will finally unify Japan once more. I believe under his rule we will bring peace to Japan for quite some time. And if that is the case, then perhaps I will join you on your ventures, ani."

Akikumo sipped his sake. "You say that every time, and yet you are still fighting in battles. I don't believe these humans will ever stop fighting with each other. Besides, if they do, then you will be out of a job. Along with Hachiman, that is."

"Well, between you and me, that kami needs a break.

He does not know when to quit."

"And neither do these humans. But yes, if humans quit fighting, you are welcome to join us in traveling for the kami."

Yamiyo slapped my back, almost causing me to spill my drink. "Isn't that marvelous news? You will have your *ojisan* with you!"

"I told you, she's not my daughter."

"But either way, I can still be her ojisan. I have already taught her the ways of sake. I'm practically there already."

Akikumo rolled his eyes as I kept sipping on my sake. I listened as they talked further on topics I didn't understand. The more I drank, the more tired I became, and suddenly their voices felt as if they were off in the distance.

CHAPTER FIFTEEN

Present day

So that was why Inari didn't want us to come this way. Now it all made sense.

I examined Yamato's wound, the stench of human blood filling my nostrils. There was no way he would be able to walk on it—at least not until we got to the hot spring. Once we arrived, I could buy something that could heal it in no time. Yokai medicine was the best; nothing the humans made could ever compare.

I sat back and looked up at Yamato. "I will need to

carry you the rest of the way."

He shook his head. "There is no way I'll let some girl carry me. I will look ridiculous."

I raised an eyebrow and gestured for him to stand up. "Fine, try to walk and see."

He stepped up on the foot and grimaced before falling back down.

"Baka. Let me carry you. Then you can focus on the map and your phone and tell me where to go."

"But aren't you weak from that attack? It looked like it took a lot out of you."

He had a point. That last attack had left me exhausted, and I didn't know how much longer I would last. I wanted to pass out at that moment, but I had to keep going.

Just think about the sake, hot spring, and aburaage, Ketsueki. It will be there, waiting for you.

Giving him my backpack, I knelt down with my back facing Yamato and held out my hands. "Go ahead and climb on me. I will be fine."

He put on both the backpacks and pulled himself up on my back as I wrapped my arms around his legs.

"As long as we don't run into any more yokai, right?"

I nodded. "Pretty much. But I think we will be okay.

The bathhouse isn't much farther, correct?"

"According to the map, it's only two more hours."

I could do that. At least I hoped so. Two hours was nothing compared to all the hours I spent traveling.

"Point which way I need to go."

"You really are clueless, aren't you? We had been heading up the hill on our way, so which way do you think we need to head?"

I sighed. "I will drop you here and go by myself."

"Of which you wouldn't know where to go because you are completely incompetent when it comes to directions."

"Which way?"

He pointed up the hill. I took a deep breath, regretting taking the shortcut. Why was I always this unlucky? I guess it all started when Akikumo left me at the Inari shrine and everything went downhill from there. It had been torture living there, as none of the kitsune liked me from the start. He expected them to befriend me and teach me everything I needed to know.

Instead, they taught me how to fight for survival and not trust anyone.

"How long have you been at the shrine?" Yamato asked, as if he knew what I was thinking about.

"Oh, just under two hundred years."

He paused. "That's a long time."

"Not for us. You humans have brief lives and don't experience time like we do."

"I suppose not."

We were quiet for a bit, and I climbed up the steep hill. Everything around me felt fuzzy, as if it was darkening, except the sun was still in the sky. I wavered a little, almost losing my footing under some gravel. I was so out of it all I could smell was Yamato's blood, which wasn't a good thing.

Focus, Ketsueki. Focus.

"Are you okay?"

I nodded. "Yeah, just tired. I will be fine though."

"Maybe we should stop so you can rest."

I shook my head. "If we stop, it is a higher chance of getting attacked by yokai. Once we get to the bathhouse, we will be fine."

"It's a yokai bathhouse, correct?"

I nodded. "Yes."

"Will I be allowed in?"

That was a good question. Had I ever seen a human in a yokai bathhouse before? Maybe once, but that was not a splendid example. I kept trying to think back to any other time. I came up with nothing.

"We will figure that out when we get there. I think you can if I am there. Just don't leave my sight, and you should be fine."

"This isn't going to be like *Sen to Chihiro no Kamikakushi* is it? I don't think I could deal with that right now."

"Like what?"

I felt him shake his head. "Never mind, forget about it. I forgot you probably don't watch movies."

"What is a movie?"

"It's like a play, but you watch it on a screen. Like my phone."

I didn't quite understand but decided not to press further. "I used to go to plays with Aki-chan. We went to some wonderful plays together, both yokai and human. It surprised me humans could be so clever."

"Tsuki-san, you don't like humans, do you?"

That was an understatement. "No, I don't."

"What happened? I presume that since you are a yokai that they tried to hurt you, sort of like all the old folklore."

My body tensed. "Something like that, yes."

"Well, I would never hurt you," he whispered. My

cheeks warmed. He was the first human that had seen my true form and didn't run away. But that didn't mean I would forgive humans that easily. No, they still had done many disastrous things in the past— things I wouldn't ever forget.

"You can call me Ketsue-chan."

"Is that what Akikumo-sama used to call you?"

I nodded. "And his otouto."

"Oh, I didn't know there was another wolf we were looking for."

I frowned, the memory of Yamiyo coming back to me. "There isn't."

"Ah. I'm sorry."

"It was a long time ago. Don't worry about it."

Yamato was quiet for a moment. "You can call me by my first name as well. I don't really have a cute nickname or anything that people call me."

I bit my lip, trying to think of something. "How about Yama-chan?"

"Whatever. Sure."

I smiled a little, glad that I had something more informal to call him. I told myself that it was because I didn't like giving humans honorifics, but after he said no one had a nickname for him and I did, that made me special, right?

Shaking my head, I pushed away any thoughts of being special. Why did I care? He was just a human I got stuck babysitting while I looked for Akikumo. I mean, he helped me travel as I didn't know where I was going, but that was it. There was nothing more.

"So, why aren't you afraid of yokai as most of the others? When humans saw them, they used to be terrified."

"I don't know. I guess I just always accepted my fate. I've seen yokai since I was tiny. Some are nice, some liked to pick on me, and some…" He trailed off as if remembering what had happened to him. "Some, like the one that attacked us, want to kill. I have never defeated any before but usually can run away and back to where my parents are. They never believed me of course, and so I stopped talking about them."

"But they still keep attaching themselves to you."

"Exactly. I don't mind them most of the time, but some can be mischievous, and since no one sees them…"

"They blame you." I finished his sentence.

"Yup. My entire life has been like that. I have told my parents many times, but they never believed me, which is funny since my father is the shrine priest. You would think he would believe in such spiritual things."

I understood why Inari wanted me to take him with me. "I think the problem is more he believes in spirits but doesn't think they are actually with you. Does that make sense?"

"Yeah, it does. It just doesn't help that he doesn't see them yet worships Inari-sama. I just don't get how someone so close to the gods can't see the surrounding spirits."

"Faith isn't seeing, faith is believing," I explained.

"Like you have faith this Akikumo is still alive?"

"It's not just faith; I know he is alive. There is no way he can be dead. He was too powerful."

"I see."

"I wonder, however, why so few humans can see yokai these days, even ones who believe in spirits. Everything just kind of stopped two centuries ago."

"Is that good or bad?"

I laughed a little. "I'm not sure, to be honest."

After an hour, we made it to where the trees started to spread out. I noticed there were more people in this area, and they kept looking at us. I presumed it was because I had Yamato on my back and women weren't supposed to carry boys.

"Um, Ketsue-chan?"

I blushed as he used that name. "Yes, Yama-chan?"

"Your ears and tails are showing."

I jumped, almost dropping Yamato. "Why didn't you say anything earlier? Humans have been staring at us!"

"Don't worry, they probably just think you are some strange cosplayer. They won't try to hurt you or anything."

"A cosplayer?" I asked.

"Someone who dresses up. A lot of humans dress up for events and wear animal ears and tails. Although yours do look a lot more real compared to those."

"That's because they are real."

"Fair. Right now no one is looking though, so you can transform."

I did just that and kept forward. "How much longer do we have?"

Yamato shifted on my back, and I did my best not to drop him. I was nearing my limit and needed to get to our destination as quick as we could.

"It should just be up ahead. Do you think you can last much longer?"

"No, but what choice do I have?"

I kept on trekking, and as I was about to collapse, I saw the sun-bleached torii we needed to pass under. I quickened my pace and prayed that since I was carrying a human, that I could take him with me as we transported into the void between this world and the netherworld.

Stepping my foot through the torii, my body transformed back into a kitsune and I felt Yamato still on my back. That was a good sign as now before us was a magnificent building. I heard Yamato gasp as he saw the scenery. On the other side of the torii, there had been nothing, but now on the top of this mountain terrain was a gigantic building that was painted every different color. It had at least seven levels. I admired it for a moment, then my body gave out.

That's when I collapsed to the ground.

CHAPTER SIXTEEN

Summer 1596 (Azuchi-Momoyama Period)—Hida Mountains

We sat at the table in Akikumo's small home, enjoying the breeze coming through the open shoji. Even up on the mountain peak, the air was hotter this time of year. I was glad it wasn't as cold as the year before, as the snow didn't want to melt and I found myself curled up under the table in my fox form more often than not. Yamiyo simply stayed warm by drinking all the liquor he could. Although even now that it was hot, he was still sipping on some sake. I guess it didn't matter what temperature it was to him.

"I will need to return to my work next month, but I have had a lot of fun joining you two on your adventures." Yamiyo grinned widely, folding his thick arms in front of himself. His long, black hair was pulled back, and his wolf ears made him appear even taller. The contrast between him and Akikumo was like night and day, but after traveling with both of them for the past few years, I saw the resemblance through their honor and loyalty to the gods and sympathy to those around them.

"Ojisan! Don't leave us!" I wrapped my arms around him and threatened not to let go.

He laughed. "Don't worry, Ketsue-chan. I'm not leaving yet. First I want to treat the two of you to somewhere special."

"Oh?" Akikumo raised an eyebrow. "And what is that? It better not be another sake bar. Ketsue-chan is not allowed the stuff anymore."

I blushed, as last time I turned into a fox and passed out. I only had one full cup.

"No, it is not a sake bar. They serve sake where we are going though, so the two of us can treat ourselves and we won't have to worry about Ketsue-chan turning into a fox."

"And what is this mysterious place?"

"In the north mountains, there is a beautiful *konyoku* that has recently opened up for yokai called Yamagami Konyoku. It's supposed to be for high-up kami and yokai, and you need a reservation a year in advance to get in." He held up three pieces of paper. "And guess who got us tickets a year ago?"

I let go of him and jumped up and down. "Yay! A yokai onsen! I can't wait!"

Akikumo patted Yamiyo on the shoulder. "Well done, otouto. I didn't think you could even surprise me."

Yamiyo smiled proudly. "Well, what's a younger brother to do when his ani is one like yourself?"

I kept jumping up and down. "When are we going to go, ojisan?"

"Tomorrow we will go to town and find us some horses and ride up north and arrive by the week's end. Then we can relax for a few days in a beautiful bathhouse."

I made a mental list of all the things I would need to bring and what I would need to buy once we arrived. I needed a new kimono for sure, as the one I wore daily was getting old. This would be the best vacation ever.

As Yamiyo predicted, we arrived at the bathhouse by the end of the week. There was a reason the place was named yamagami as the building literally stood on the top of Mount Odake. By the time we reached the peak where the torii gate awaited, I was out of breath and ready to relax in the hot water that awaited me. We had to sell the horses lower on the mountain as they wouldn't have been able to make it to this area.

"We are here!" Yamiyo clapped his hands together.

I collapsed dramatically and curled up in a ball.

Akikumo rolled his eyes. "I'm not carrying you, Ketsue-chan. Don't even try it."

Reaching down, Yamiyo lifted me up into his arms. "I will! Otherwise what kind of ojisan would I be?"

I gave Akikumo a look of triumph, and the three of us walked through the torii gate. I stared in astonishment at the grand building that lay before me. Yamiyo was right; this was definitely a new building. It appeared pristine and glistened in the summer sun.

The building spanned the top of the mountain and comprised three large levels. It was busy, exactly as Yamiyo had mentioned. A *rokurokubi* walked in front of us, his neck stretching high into the sky. I hadn't seen one in quite a while and gaped at him. I wondered how he didn't have neck problems from the strain of his head.

We entered the main building, and Yamiyo set me down and spoke with the head staff. I stayed next to Akikumo, still amazed by all the yokai that wandered around. Never had I seen so many at an onsen before. The bath would be crowded more than normal, but between Yamiyo and Akikumo, I doubted anyone would give us trouble or come near us.

Yamiyo finished talking to the head staff, and an attendant joined him. The attendant was a *jorogumo* with eight spider arms that came out of her back that seemed to come in handy when helping guests carry luggage. She wore a black-and-red kimono decorated with webs. Her black eyes met mine, giving me a chill. Although here they were pleasant creatures, some weren't so friendly. And I didn't care for spiders.

Yamiyo waved us over. "Come on, we can check into our room now and change for the bath."

Akikumo and I followed Yamiyo and the jorogumo to our room. We were on the third level, which excited me because I enjoyed being on the top floor of a building as then I didn't hear anyone above us. The room was simple, with three futons rolled up and ready to be used. The room flooring was the typical tatami mats and shoji that led to the deck. Currently it was open, letting in the cool mountain air. I could see down the valley of the mountain where the human settlements were. Even though we were between dimensions, part of each world was visible until you traveled deeper into the netherworld.

The jorogumo bowed and left us in our room. Yamiyo clapped his hands together. "Well, should we go enjoy the bath?"

I nodded, unable to wait for the warm water to soothe my aching muscles. Akikumo sighed. "I suppose if you insist."

We put our things away and hurried to the bath. It was all outside, and the cool air felt nice on my skin. I wrapped my hair up with a tie, as did Akikumo and Yamiyo. We each washed ourselves with the buckets of water before entering, as is custom to clean yourselves before stepping into the water. Although for human onsen, it was custom not to let hair touch the water, it was a little more complicated for yokai. Some yokai had forms that had hair covering all or parts of their body, such as our tails. We still kept our long hair up as it was a bother to dry it, even though our tails got wet.

The onsen was a lot less crowded than I expected it would be, but there were still a lot of yokai filling up the area. Most kept their eyes to themselves, as it was a mixed gender bath. I never cared, as everyone was respectful in the yokai baths. Humans, on the other hand, I had to always keep close to Akikumo just in case.

Dipping a toe in, my body relaxed. The bath was so warm compared to the mountain air. I found a corner and sat down, enjoying the view from the top of the mountain. The valley of trees was lush. I sighed, looking down at them.

"What's that sigh for?" Yamiyo took a seat next to me.

Akikumo joined us. "She is probably wishing that the onsen was in the middle of the woods."

I blushed, although it was hard to tell as I was already heating up. "This place is marvelous. I love being in the forest."

Yamiyo laughed. "Such a fox. I will have to disagree, however, as mountaintops are much better."

I rolled my eyes. "Wolves and their mountains. It's

much colder up here if you haven't noticed."

"Then you can really appreciate the hot spring."

I leaned back and closed my eyes. "Whatever. I'd rather be where it's warm all the time."

"Doesn't your fur get too hot to deal with?"

I shook my head. "Nope. I love it."

"It's true." Akikumo sighed. "She loves the heat."

"Ten men, ten colors, I suppose. Everyone has a different favorite thing."

"Yeah, but in Ketsue-chan's case, she's just strange."

I opened an eye and stuck my tongue out at Akikumo. More yokai had joined the onsen, and for the most part, it was quiet with just a few whispering. I relaxed a bit, trying not to drift to sleep.

"Care if we join you over here?" I heard a squeak of a voice ask. I opened my eyes to find a group of small kappa standing before us.

Akikumo gestured. "It is a public bath; go right ahead."

They each nodded. "Thank you."

There were five of them, and they all appeared young. They had small beaks and black hair almost as black as Yamiyo's. They all possessed a bald spot on their head and green skin. They paddled over to a spot with their webbed hands.

"A white okami. You are a rare yokai. You don't happen to be Akikumo?" one of the kappa asked.

Akikumo nodded. "That I am."

The kappa's face lit up. "I am so glad to have run into you. We need your assistance. One of our ponds we frequent is covered in a dark miasma, and no one has succeeded in clearing it."

"Where is the pond?" he asked.

"It is in the Okayama providence."

That was clear across Japan. We had finally found time to rest, was Akikumo really considering journeying all the way to the south part of this country? I glanced over to find him thinking about it. He nodded.

"Yes, I can go there."

"Can you go as soon as possible? Many of our friends are getting sick from the miasma."

"Yes, we can. Let me stop by my home and get some things before journeying to your home."

"Thank you so much, Akikumo-sama! You are a lifesaver!"

I lowered farther in the bath, hiding the fact that I was disappointed he agreed to it. Yamiyo was leaving us soon and hoped we could stay together for a bit.

"Chin up, Ketsue-chan," Yamiyo whispered. "That is the direction I need to go so we can stay together longer. Then you will have ani all to yourself."

I smiled a little, but we both knew that wasn't true. Akikumo would always put others before himself even if it meant putting something before me.

CHAPTER SEVENTEEN

Present day—Hida Mountains

"Ketsue-chan… wake up, Ketsue-chan…"

My eyes flickered open to find Yamato's face above mine. His eyes were wide and almost red as if he had been crying. I glanced around and found myself in a ryokan room. A table full of food lay in the middle of the room. My stomach grumbled.

Yamato laughed. "Seriously? You pass out and when you wake up, your body just thinks about food?"

I nodded as I rolled over toward it. "I passed out

because I ran out of energy. Of course I am hungry."

"Well, it should still be warm. They just brought it in."

I grabbed an onigiri and stuffed it in my mouth. The center was filled with grilled salmon. I devoured it and stuffed another in my mouth.

"What happened?" Part of the journey came back to me. We had arrived at the bathhouse after climbing up the mountain. A couple of yokai then attacked us, and we barely made it out alive. "Is your leg okay?"

Yamato nodded as he leaned back. He appeared tired but had stayed awake waiting for me to be conscious once again. His once stylish hair was a mess, and his pant leg was soaked with blood, now cut above where his wound was.

"Yeah, some of the attendants here wrapped it with some plants, and the wound's almost done healing. I didn't even think that was possible."

"Plants of the yokai world are a lot more potent." I chomped on another onigiri. "Have you eaten?"

"No, I should." He took a seat next to me, and we ate in silence. There were many bowls and plates that displayed a mixture of fish, stew, vegetables cooked in many different ways, sushi, and onigiri. Sadly there was no aburaage.

Everything tasted heavenly though—fresh and filling. I would order again after we spent some time in the bath, along with some sake. I deserved it.

Leaning back, I took a deep breath. "Okay, now that we have restored our strength, tell me what happened after I passed out. How did you manage to get this room, let alone survive this place without me?"

Yamato sighed as he laid his back on the tatami map and covered his eyes with his arm. "It wasn't easy. Luckily you were in your kitsune form instead of your human form. I told them I was your human servant, and you needed care."

"Quick thinking."

"Yeah, but it took a while for them to believe me. A few were drooling on me. It was terrifying."

I laughed a little. "Well, you are safe now you have me here."

"Just don't pass out again."

"I will try my best. Now, shall we head to the baths?"

He leaned up on his arms. "Will they even let a human like me in?"

I shrugged. "Only one way to find out."

"Ugh. Well, a bath sounds good. Except you won't be

there to save me if something goes wrong."

"That's where you are wrong. This is a konyoku."

His eyes widened. "A mixed bath? I don't know if I feel comfortable…"

"Do you want to stay here by yourself?"

Yamato didn't hesitate. "Fine, I'll come."

Yamato stared at the ground, already beet red before stepping outside where the bath was. I took off my towel and pinned up my hair. I used a bucket to rinse myself off and stepped into the water.

"The water's nice and warm, Yamato, come join me!"

He reluctantly washed off and stepped into the water, his hands blocking any wandering eyes. I giggled as he moved toward me.

"This is really awkward."

I gestured around. "At least there aren't that many yokai. Usually there are many, many beings filling the bath." Actually, I noticed there weren't that many yokai in general as we walked through the building. It seemed like only a third of the rooms were occupied.

"Is it due to less human interaction with yokai?"

"I suppose… Maybe they all have moved into the netherworld. They say once you move there, you can never go back to the human world. These onsen are the only link, and then you have to choose."

"Why don't yokai just stay in the netherworld then? If humans aren't there, wouldn't they be happier?"

I shrugged. "It's not quite the same. It's kind of like the afterlife and isn't as full of life, so to speak. The human world is where all the energy and interesting stuff happens."

"I guess that makes sense. Kind of like being in the city versus the country. What about you? Do you want to stay in the human world then?"

"Of course. That is where Aki-chan is."

"What if he went to the netherworld? Would you follow him?"

I leaned back more and pursed my lips. I hadn't really thought about it, but I wondered what life would be like living in the netherworld. The place seemed so bland, but it was something I would do for him, if given the opportunity. "I suppose. But I doubt he ever would. I mean, he was created to be a link between the kami and humans. If something were to happen to him, I think it would be into a different world, not the yokai netherworld."

"Your world is complicated."

"That it is."

I leaned back and closed my eyes, taking in the warm water. Although we had a hot spring at the Inari shrine for all the kitsune, it wasn't the same as this place. The water felt warmer, purer, and more relaxing. Perhaps it had to do with the fact I had just defeated a couple of yokai.

Either way, this place was worth it.

I sat against the rock, my eyes closed, breathing in the nice clear air. I was happy the human miasma hadn't affected the air here yet. It seemed to me it was only a matter of time, but I could have been mistaken. We were on the border of the netherworld after all; it wasn't like humans could visit here.

Hopefully it would stay that way.

Peering over at Yamato, I found him resting his eyes. It was good to see he was finally relaxed after everything we had gone through. For me, it wasn't anything new, but for him all of this was probably terrifying. This will help him rest well tonight before we ventured farther up the mountain. We had a long road ahead of us, especially since I didn't quite remember where Akikumo's house was. Everything kept changing through the years, and I swore the house changed spots every time we came back here. Knowing Akikumo, perhaps it did.

I heard footsteps come up to the bath.

"May we join you?" a voice asked.

Looking up, I found a group of kappas. This seemed familiar. "You may."

"Thank you. You are most kind."

The group stepped in and I sensed Yamato's worry. I leaned over and whispered in his ear.

"Don't worry, they won't steal your shirikodama."

His face turned even redder than it was from the hot water. I laughed and leaned back again. The bath was rather large, and the kappa stayed on the other side, whispering to each other. I almost drifted off, and I tried to do my best in keeping conscious as I didn't want to fall asleep in the water. I couldn't do that to Yamato.

"Miss, may we ask you a question?" a kappa squeaked.

I opened one of my eyes and looked over. Afraid it had to do with Yamato, I swam to be between him and the kappa. "What is it?"

"Were you not the kitsune that used to travel with Akikumo-sama?"

Were these the same kappa that had requested

Akikumo to help them all those years ago? "I am. Do you know where he is?"

The kappa seemed hesitant. "It has been years, but we were the ones who spotted him and reported to Inari-sama. However, we haven't seen him come down from the mountain in quite some time and fear the worst."

I shook my head. "No, if he died I would have known. Please, tell me where you saw him last."

"We met him here a while back again, and he said he was heading home up the mountains, nestled in between Mount Tate and Mount Tsurugi. You will have a lengthy journey before you, going up those mountains, not to mention the evil yokai in the area seem to be getting more restless."

This we already knew. "Thank you. That gives us at least a direction as to where to go."

"If you find him, please send him our regards. We are thankful for all the help he has given the kappas in his life. We will never forget his generosity."

No, it seemed like no one ever forgot all the things he did for them, even the humans. Yet they all thought he was dead. It made no sense. If they thought something happened, why did no one look for him? Or help? Why was I the only one who searched for the person who has kept this world going?

He had to be alive. I could feel it in my chest. His energy still existed. I wouldn't let anyone tell me otherwise.

Yamato and I retired back to our room, and I lay on my side, sipping my sake and looking out into the mountainside. Now I knew where his home was, and we could head straight there in the morning. The mountains were still beautiful even if humans were slowly expanding their city. I took a deep breath, relishing in the clean air.

"Is it wise to drink sake?"

I glanced over where Yamato was sitting, his arms wrapped around his legs, keeping his beige after-bath kimono tight, as if afraid it would come loose and I would see him naked again. "I won't get drunk. I built up a tolerance eventually. Besides, I will only have a couple of cups."

"Ah."

"You should try some."

"I'm underage."

"I suppose for human society you are. But remember,

you are in a yokai onsen. Those rules don't apply here."

He shook his head. "I shouldn't."

"You are telling me a delinquent like you hasn't been drinking?"

"I just mostly get into fights, and I have found that people who drink don't fight as well."

He had a point. I had seen many men stumble while trying to throw a punch, only to fall. "That's fair. However, this is yokai sake. It's not the same as human sake. This might be your only chance to have some."

Yamato hesitated as I handed him a cup. He slowly took a sip and his eyes brightened. "Sugoi, this is amazing!"

I chuckled. "I told you so. But only that cup. Who knows if you can hold your liquor?"

"That's fair."

I finished my glass and held up the blue magatama. I was very close to finding him now. I would have my answers at last.

"What is that?" Yamato asked.

I let out a sigh. "A gift from Aki-chan. It's the only thing I have of his. He gave it to me, saying it was the same color as my fire."

"That sounds precious."

"It is. If anything happened to it, I don't know what I would do."

Yamato didn't answer, and as I peered over at him, I found him asleep. I got up and moved my sake so I could roll out the futons. I placed him in his and blew out the candles. We needed to rest if we were going to hike to the next mountain tomorrow.

CHAPTER EIGHTEEN

Winter 1596 (Azuchi-Momoyama Period)—Okayama Providence

I really hated snow. Even with my fur the cold was miserable. I wrapped my three tails around myself, trying to block the white coldness from touching my kimono and haori. It felt like my nose hairs were frozen. I missed the nice, warm summer months and couldn't wait for them to come back.

I watched as Akikumo walked in front of me with ease, as if the coldness meant nothing to him. We had gone up to the pond the kappas needed help with. After Akikumo cleared the area for them, they begged him to stay the summer… which led into fall… and now we were into winter, heading down the mountains to get where it was a bit warmer, after much pleading on my end.

Normally, before I came around, Yamiyo revealed Akikumo stayed in the snowcapped mountains during the winter. If it weren't for me, he wouldn't have traveled down the mountain to the coast, or anywhere warmer really. I felt bad about having changed Akikumo's routine, but I also didn't want to stay.

We parted ways with Yamiyo a few months back once we'd reached the pond. I missed him already, but Akikumo assured me that once he was done with his work, he would rejoin us. I couldn't wait until I had my ojisan back. I cared about Akikumo a lot, but I enjoyed having Yamiyo around. Akikumo opened up more with his brother, and I enjoyed seeing that side of him.

We trekked down the mountainside, and I wrapped my arms around myself even tighter. Akikumo didn't look over at me, knowing what I would say.

"This is why I was begging you to leave earlier, Aki-chan. Now we are stuck in the snow. I don't want to camp out another night in my fox form."

Akikumo sighed. "Then we will find the closest human settlement and stay in a hotel."

"But I don't want to stay with the humans."

"Then we should have stayed with the kappa."

"But it was cold up there."

Akikumo turned and gave me a look. "Well you will have to decide here real soon as we are halfway down the mountain."

I pouted. "Well… we should have left earlier and none of this would have been a problem."

"Yes, you've said that. But we couldn't be disrespectful to the kappas' hospitality."

"They were the ones who were disrespectful to you by not letting you leave and demanding you stop your plans and travel across Japan to help them with something they should have fixed themselves."

Wrapping his arms around me, Akikumo stroked my back. "Oh, Ketsue-chan. You have much to learn about humility and generosity."

"But they aren't being generous to you! They are just using you."

"That doesn't matter. If I was only generous to people who were generous back, then it wouldn't mean a thing."

"But shouldn't there be an equal exchange between two people? It doesn't seem fair."

"Nothing in this world is fair, but we must always strive to be good. Otherwise, there wouldn't be a point, now would there?"

I frowned. "I guess not."

He stepped back and smiled. "Now, where do you want to go?"

I played with the snow using my geta. "Down the mountain toward the human settlement. But I think you should be generous to me and get me some apples preserved in honey."

"At this time of year? That will cost a lot."

"Well, you should have left the mountain earlier."

He laughed as he ruffled the top of my head. "Never change Ketsue-chan. Now, we better keep going so we can get there before dark. I don't want to hear you complain how cold it is once the sun sets."

"Then you better get walking."

The snow came down more violently, and we found ourselves in the middle of a blizzard. We couldn't stop as then we wouldn't reach the town before the sun set, but it was difficult to see much ahead of us. Everything was painted white, and the wind howled through the forest, almost as powerful as a demon.

Akikumo didn't slow down from this snow but seemed to relish in it. Maybe Yamiyo was right—Akikumo really loved the snowy winter. I felt bad for making him always leave the mountain. There were times we had stayed for a bit, but it was never for the entire summer. I couldn't ever understand why he enjoyed it so much as my fur was beginning to freeze.

Glancing up at Akikumo, I found that his white fur blended in with the snow. Perhaps that was why he liked it so much—this was where he was supposed to be. I never wanted to leave Akikumo's side, but I also didn't enjoy forcing him to travel when he didn't want to. I wanted to tell him I was sorry for being selfish, but I was afraid if I opened my mouth, it would freeze. I would just have to tell him later.

We came upon a small clearing where the trees didn't shield us from most of the snowstorm, and I felt as if I were getting whipped by the wind. How could snow be so soft yet so powerful?

Akikumo stopped right in front of me and I slammed into him. I glanced up to see what was wrong, when I noticed his ears twitched and he placed his hand on his katana. I tried to listen, but all I could hear was the wind howling. I took a deep breath and let my mind calm some more, when I picked it up—the faint cry of a woman.

Akikumo started forward in the direction that the voice was coming from, and I followed suit. As we walked a few steps forward, her figure appeared in the snowstorm. She wore a white kimono, almost like a wedding kimono. Her hair was long and dark black, sprawling all around her as she sat in the middle of the snow.

As we came closer, she moved her kimono sleeves away from her face. Her eyes were red, as she had been crying, but her skin was a pasty white. It almost appeared as if she had thick makeup on, but her skin didn't seem to be covered in any substance.

Akikumo knelt beside her, his hand still on his katana. "What is wrong?"

"My husband. He is gone." She started crying again, burrowing her face into her sleeves.

I glanced around to find any evidence of the husband and saw a mound in the snow. I dug a little to find a man. His face was turning a shade of blue, but his chest was still moving.

"Aki-chan! I found him!"

Picking the man up by the arms, I dragged him to where the woman was. "He is still alive. Your husband is not gone."

She kept on crying, as if not listening to what I had said.

Akikumo took a deep breath. "This is not your husband, is it?"

She shook her head. "No, it is not."

"Then why were you crying next to his body?"

I didn't like where this was going, not to mention this man needed to get somewhere warm if he was going to survive. But did I care? My own concern surprised me, but I didn't pay it much mind. I would just see what Akikumo wanted to do.

She peered up at Akikumo. "You don't understand. These men always come and they always try to take me away somewhere else. They don't know what it is like to have lost someone they loved. All they want to do is keep me for themselves. Since they don't understand true agony, they have paid the price for their sins for not listening."

It hit me. She was a ghost yokai, forever wandering this forest because of her husband's death. I wondered how she died and if she had frozen out here in the mountains. It would make sense, given the blizzard.

Akikumo reached his hand out and grabbed hers. "I will listen to you tell of your husband. Who was he? What happened?"

The ghost yokai's eyes widened, as if surprised by the gesture. "He was an excellent man. He provided for me and protected me. We used to live out in these woods when a big snowstorm hit. He was outside getting firewood when a tree fell on him."

"What did you do?"

Tears ran down her face. "I wept over his body and never left it, becoming one with the snow. I never left him."

"Then what are you doing out here? Should you not go to the other side so you can be with your husband there?"

"But I can't leave this place. The town nearby—it was their fault we had to live in the forest. They cast us out when we were poor and needed help. I will never forgive them."

"So you wait for men to come out here, cause a large snowstorm, and bury them beneath the snow?"

She nodded. "It's what they deserve."

Akikumo shook his head. "No, these aren't the men who did you wrong. These are innocent men. You must move on. Do you want me to help you move on?"

The woman appeared as if she was giving what he proposed much thought. No one had ever given her the chance to move on, and she must have forgotten how. "Please."

Standing up, Akikumo bowed, clapped his hands together twice, and bowed once more. Suddenly the woman became snowflakes and was taken by the wind. Akikumo took a deep breath and let it out slowly.

"Thank you," a voice whispered. I glanced all around but didn't see any sign of the woman. She had moved on.

Turning to the human, Akikumo lifted him up and placed him on his back to carry. "Let's go, Ketsue-chan. We need to get this man somewhere warm."

I followed him as he headed back into the forest. "Why did you help the ghost if she was hurting people?"

"Her heart was in the right place. She missed her husband and got lost. I simply helped her find her way."

"Why are you helping this man then? It seems that he only wanted to talk to the ghost because she was a beautiful woman."

"Even so, he doesn't deserve to die. And remember before when I said we were to be generous to others?"

I did. "Do you think if this man survives and we get him to town, they will be generous and give us honey-preserved apples?"

Akikumo rolled his eyes.

CHAPTER NINETEEN

Present day—Hida Mountains

We rested well at the onsen and woke at sunrise to head back out for the day. Yamato located the peaks of Mount Tate and Tsurugi, and we highlighted the area between the two mountains where Akikumo's home could be. I knew the building had to be above the tree level, as Akikumo loved the mountaintops. Once our hike was planned, we made our way over the mountain.

The closest mountain to us was Mount Gaki. Once we were on the top, I could get a better look of the area and see if I remember anything. Hopefully I would, but as Yamato pointed out, I was not good with directions.

I never noticed before as I always had someone else with me and I didn't have to worry about which way we were headed. Now that I was on my own and out of the safety of the shrine, I was completely confused.

"How is your leg?" I asked Yamato as he led us up the mountainside. He wore similar clothes to the day before, but they were a different color. Now he wore a red button-down shirt over a white T-shirt and light jeans. I still wore my white-and-blue yukata, as I was used to wearing the same thing for a few days of traveling at a time.

He shrugged. "It's fine. The wound closed before we went into the bath last night, and any soreness was gone when I woke up."

"That's yokai medicine for you."

"If humans had such efficient medicine, there would be much more peace."

I laughed. "Really? You think so? I doubt any of that would change humans. I think it would make them more lazy as they didn't have consequences to their actions."

"I suppose that is true. Although not all illnesses

result from one's choice."

"But it is the result of humans as a whole. That's where everything will go downhill, then the people would pay the price for that."

"You have a point there."

We reached the top of the mountain, and I gazed out on the valleys. The lush forest surrounded us and filled in the spaces between the peaks. I caught glimpses of lakes and rivers. There might be a few rivers we would have to find a way to get across. That would be a future problem we would solve once we got there.

After yesterday's fiasco, I decided it would be easier to stay in my kitsune form and listen for humans and change back if need be. I didn't want any yokai to have the upper hand out there, not when we were so close.

Yamato pointed. "Our best bet is to head toward Mount Harinoki and stay the night near the top. Then tomorrow we can climb down to the Kurobe River, make our way around the dam, and head up Mount Tate first. From there we can hike up Mount Tsurugi. We will have to go around the dam or else we will come upon more humans than we want."

"No humans, please."

"Which is why we will have to go way around. I

think it will be fine though. These are enormous mountains."

"Lead the way." I gestured forward.

Walking across these mountains reminded me of all the traveling Akikumo and I did while we were together. I didn't realize how much I missed those adventures until I found myself out here with Yamato. I had been so alone at the Inari shrine that having even a human traveling with me felt refreshing. It was strange to think this was my outcome after years of wanting to get away from all humans in general. Akikumo would be proud once he saw me.

Mount Gaki was a lot more rocky than I remembered, although I had been on so many mountaintops that I was losing count and meshed most together. Most of Japan was like that, which made it hard for humans to use a lot of the land. I was thankful for this as it meant my habitat was still there. I took in a big breath of the mountain air and said thanks to the kami as they had blessed us with sunshine. Anything was better than the winter months here, however, as I remembered their bitter bite when the snow fell, until spring came and melted away the snow. It fascinated me how different this land could look between summer and winter.

Making our way down the mountain and into the valley, I noticed we were coming upon a road that had vehicles racing by. I turned into my human form.

"There are roads like this all the way out here?" I asked as we walked up to the human structure.

Yamato nodded. "Yup. That way humans can reach some of the onsen and camping sites easier."

I shook my head. "Wouldn't it be much more of an accomplishment if they did it all on their own without a vehicle?"

"I suppose. But many don't have the time or the physical fitness for such activities."

"Then they should climb more mountains."

Yamato laughed. "And get attacked by yokai?"

"Fair point. It is just strange seeing so many humans out here though. It used to only be us yokai."

Once we crossed the road, we stopped for lunch. I sat on a log and pulled out my onigiri that I'd gotten from the onsen. Munching on the rice, I took a quick look around. Why did this not seem as familiar as it should have? Had that much time passed?

"Still feel lost?" Yamato asked as he ate his lunch.

I shrugged. "Not so much lost as confused. I can't believe how much time has passed still. It has been jarring."

"I suppose that would be strange. I can't imagine being alive that long and witnessing everything that you have."

I nodded. I had met so many yokai, kami, and humans over the years, and many of them had passed on to the next world. I didn't even want to try to figure out what the numbers would be.

We finished our meal and started off again. Hours passed as we pushed ourselves up the mountain. Soon we came to the top of Mount Harinoki. The wind was powerful as we stood at the very peak. The sun was beginning to set, and the sky appeared to be painted in swathes of reds, oranges, and pinks. I stretched.

"We made it!"

Yamato collapsed on the ground. "That we did!"

"You should put up your tent before it gets dark. I will start a fire."

He nodded as he rolled over and unpacked his bag. As I readied the fire with some sticks I had gathered on the way up the mountain, I watched in amazement how fast Yamato set up his tent.

"Wow, you are pretty good at that."

He nodded. "Yeah, we used to go hiking a lot when I

was a child. We haven't for a long time though, but I guess this part stuck with me."

"How was that? Especially since you could see yokai?"

He shrugged as he took a seat by the fire. "I did fine. Sleeping in my tent alone was the worst as I heard things all night, but my parents didn't hear anything. Luckily there were a lot of humans around so there weren't any big problems. It was mainly little ones that tried to play tricks on me."

"Lucky for you. But that must have been traumatizing as a child. I'm surprised you aren't afraid of them all." As I used to be with humans. Yet he went on with dealing with them. I supposed it was because no one believed him.

"I was at first, but as time went on, I decided it was fine as long as I didn't interact with them and kept my distance. Then I gave them food when they wanted it. I am actually a pretty talented cook, might I add."

"Are you now? Well, you will have to prove that to me later, otherwise I won't believe you."

"Are you going to go back to Kyoto after you find Akikumo though? I would figure you would want to stay with him."

He had a point. I didn't want to go anywhere that Akikumo wasn't. "I will see if he will come to Kyoto with me, and then I will show up at your door, demanding food."

Yamato laughed. "I could see that. You seem to love food a lot. Speaking of which, should we get that package of soup going?"

I nodded. "Yes, let's."

Yamato pulled out the package of soup he had brought and filled a small pot with water. "This doesn't count as my cooking, for the record. Packaged soup never tastes as good as the genuine thing."

"I haven't had it either way."

"I guess you wouldn't have if you haven't left the mountain for decades. Well, be ready to be disappointed."

As he set up the pot above the fire, he kept glancing over at me. I cocked my head a little. "What's wrong?"

"It's just… I was wondering if I could pet your tails. They look really soft, and I have been curious. What a real kitsune tail feels like."

I blushed and fidgeted a little. "I haven't ever had someone ask me that. I don't know…"

He held up his hands. "Sorry, I didn't mean to make

it awkward. I just was curious, that's all."

I bit my lip. "No, it's fine. Go ahead and pet it. I keep my tails clean and as fluffy as they can be. You won't find better tails than mine."

Yamato stepped closer and stroked my tail. It felt strange to have a human touch my tail, but I knew he didn't mean anything by it. If I met a creature with such gorgeous tails, I would want to pet them as well.

"It's super soft!"

I smiled smugly. "Yeah, I know."

"Are they all this soft?"

"Of course. What kind of kitsune would I be if I didn't keep them looking like they do?"

"I hear Ichika-san berated you about not keeping your kimono in pristine condition. I guess I assumed you didn't care about your looks as much as the others."

"That's a bit different. My tails are my pride and joy whereas my clothing is not. As you can see…" I gestured to my kimono that had been snagged a few times from branches and slashed from the yokai we had faced. "Traveling does a number on my clothing, but I can always get a new kimono. I can't get a new tail."

"I guess that makes sense."

After a little while, the soup was ready. I blew on it a bit and took a sip. Yamato was right; this was not the best soup in the world, as it was quite salty, but it still tasted fine after a long day of hiking.

"Well." Yamato gathered my bowl and put away the equipment. "I think we should retire for the night. Are you not going to sleep in a tent?"

I shook my head as I transformed into a fox. "I like to sleep in my fox form while in the wilderness."

He looked at me a bit surprised I had transformed so quickly. "I guess that makes sense. Well then, good night."

"Good night, Yama-chan." I curled up in a ball and tried to fall asleep. All I could think about was the fact that tomorrow it was possible I could see Akikumo again. And the fact that we hadn't run into any yokai.

Which meant tomorrow something would happen, whether it be good or bad.

CHAPTER TWENTY

Summer 1611 (Edo Period)—Edo

As we stepped out of the forest, I couldn't believe my eyes. There were crowds of men and women, traveling on a road that seemed to lead toward Edo. I held on to Akikumo's cotton kimono, wondering where they all were coming from.

"Why are there so many people? I have never seen so many travel before that didn't have to do with war."

Akikumo chuckled as he moved and tucked his white hair behind his ear. "Well, it seems humans are doing more trade between cities and have created a road between Kyoto and Edo."

I frowned. I did not like the fact that humans were traveling like this. It meant they were impeding into our territory. Now yokai couldn't come around these parts without humans seeing them and starting a hunt. I clutched Akikumo's warm hand, not wanting to stray far with all these humans around. His skin was warm and comforting, and I always felt safe when I was close to him. There was nothing to fear when Akikumo was around.

We came upon a narrowing passage with a wooden fence. There were a few men and women stopping people and talking to them. We got in line, and I clutched Akikumo's kimono some more. He patted my head.

"It will be fine. They are just making sure that no one is coming to cause problems. As you can see, no one can carry a weapon except samurai, who are trained warriors. And, of course, me."

"Are they really afraid of their own kind like that? Doesn't it seem strange?"

"Well, you won't even go talk to your own kind when you see them, so I don't think you have room to talk.

Besides, this country is enormous and there are a lot of different types of humans, just like there are yokai."

He made a fair point, and I decided to let it go. These humans wouldn't ever really make sense to me anyway.

I stuck close to him, however, as I still didn't trust these humans. They did nothing to cause me to change that opinion. As we came closer to the gate, I noticed the air seem to get thicker, and it felt hard to breathe. What was this miasma? Why was it so thick there?

Akikumo glanced down at me, as if seeing if I also noticed the stench. "Do you smell that, Ketsue-chan?"

I nodded. "It reeks of mold and valerian."

Akikumo chuckled. "That is a suitable way to describe it. You and I are used to the mountain and forest air, and it seems the more humans expand, the more evil energy seems to collect in the cities."

"Which proves my point that they are evil beings."

"Or maybe they have more hardships than you and me. The best plants grow in the harshest conditions."

"So you say."

We stopped our conversation as we reached the front of the line, and the samurai guard started barking out questions.

"Why are you visiting Edo?"

"We are simply humble travelers wanting to see the capital and buy a gift for our friends," Akikumo replied gently.

"How long will you be staying?"

"For a few days."

"Do you know anyone in Edo?"

"No."

The samurai crossed his arms, as if still suspicious of us. Akikumo, however, kept his cool.

"Where are you going to stay?" the guard asked.

"At a hotel."

"Do you have enough money to pay for a hotel?"

"Of course."

"Are you on the run from law enforcements in the neighboring towns?"

"No."

The samurai gestured to the gate. "You may enter."

We walked past him and entered the town. The stench was even stronger inside, and I covered my nose with my kimono sleeve.

Once we were out of hearing range of the samurai, I leaned over and whispered, "How did he not notice your katana?"

"It is because of my sugure. I hid it from him."

I forgot Akikumo could hide objects using his sugure. I still needed to get better at it, although I could hide my ears and tails easily now.

Peering around, I found there were a lot more buildings here than I had ever imagined possible. Was this how all the towns would eventually be? There were so many humans walking around and many samurai, who seemed to be the law enforcement of the area, that I worried what if I accidentally transformed into my kitsune self? Would there be a way out of here? I glanced around. No, it would be near impossible. I didn't believe I could escape.

"I don't want to be here, Aki-chan. What if I mess up?"

"You will be fine. I am here to keep you safe, remember? I won't let anything happen to you."

"I guess."

He placed his hand on my shoulder. "Now, let us get some food and look around to see what these humans have been up to lately."

Akikumo led us to a ramen shop. We passed under the cloth banners, and the scent of broth instantly hit me. I was drooling before I ordered my ramen, with a topping of fried tofu of course. They didn't take long to serve it, and I savored the meal. It was one of the best ramen bowls I had ever eaten. At least humans were getting better at cooking. Maybe I could stay around them if they kept this up.

Once we were finished, Akikumo led us out of the shop and toward the textile area. Men and women adored kimonos and haori as they lined the streets. Most were made of cotton, but they now made many of a finer material that I had seen some kami wear. Humans must have started designing things more intricately just like we yokai had been doing for centuries. Maybe one day they could catch up to us.

"Do you like any of these?"

I pondered the question. Many of them were unique. I stepped up to one of the kimonos that was a shade of blue unlike anything I had seen before. As I examined it more, I found that it slowly faded into a pink color at the bottom of the kimono. The fade was so natural that I hadn't even noticed. "This one is pretty."

"Of course you pick the most expensive one. Would you like it?"

I nodded. "Yes please."

Akikumo pulled out his string of coins and handed the merchant a couple. The man bowed, and Akikumo took the kimono off the hanger and folded it up. "Well, shall we get a room where we can store this there?"

"Yeah! And then we can go get some apples in honey."

He let out a lengthy breath. "You are addicted to those, aren't you?"

"Yes!"

"Fine, we can go look for some since they are in season. I'm surprised you haven't begged me for aburaage lately."

"That will be for dinner of course. It goes without saying."

"Of course it does."

We wandered around the merchant area and looked at the paintings and jewelry before heading toward the hotel. My eye caught a pendant that looked similar to Akikumo's.

I pointed at it. "Is that the same pendant you wear?"

He nodded. "In looks, yes, but mine has a lot more meaning than that one."

"Oh? Like what?"

He patted my head. "I will tell you once we get to the hotel."

We made it to the hotel, which sat close to the bay,

looking out over the ocean. The blue water sparkled in the summer sun. I smiled as the salty wind caressed my long black and red hair, wishing I could enjoy this without so many humans around. Next stop, we would stay at a beach that didn't have any humans. I would beg for it.

Akikumo gave the hostess a few coins from his string, and she led us down the hallway and up the stairs to the top floor. I smiled when seeing we had a room that faced the water. Once the hostess left us, Akikumo laid out the kimono and took a seat by the shoji that faced toward the ocean.

"Come sit with me, and I will tell you a story."

I set my things down and took a seat next to Akikumo, breathing in the salty air. I wished days like this would last forever. The air was a perfect temperature, and even though there was a lot of miasma in the city, facing the ocean like this made the air a lot more pleasant. I could even breath now without smelling that foul stench. I wished we could stay in here and not interact with the humans again for the day, but we still needed dinner.

Akikumo untied his necklace and held up the pendant. "This pendant is called a magatama. A long time ago, the kami Susanoo-sama had five hundred of these made to give to his sister Amaterasu-sama. He did this to please her as he often got on her bad side, between his partying and lack of respect to her home. Amaterasu-sama then used the magatama to create gods, and each god possessed one of these magatama, representing their ki."

"So it contains your ki?"

"I was created before they passed these out, so I do not need it to control my ki. It was more given as a gift so we all were connected." He paused for a moment, then held out the necklace. "How about you take it for now?"

I widened my eyes. "But this is your ki! They gave it to you by one of the most significant kami in Japan. I can't accept something so important to you."

"I insist. That way if we ever get separated, you will always have a part of me. And then I will be able to find you as I know at all times where that magatama is."

I blushed as I took the magatama. "I will always cherish this."

"And it matches your kitsunebi and your new kimono. You will look beautiful."

"I guess I will have to show off both tonight when we

go out for aburaage and honey apples."

He raised an eyebrow. "Do you always think of food, Ketsue-chan?"

I nodded. "Yes!"

CHAPTER TWENTY-ONE

Present Day—Hida Mountains

Today was a lot warmer than I planned for, but it still beat the snow.

Sweat soaked my yukata as we descended the mountain toward the Kurobe River. I kept an ear out for humans but had heard none. I glanced over at Yamato, who had seemed to be doing all this rigorous climbing rather well. The Hida Mountains weren't the easiest terrain to master.

He must have noticed me watching him as he turned

to glance at me. "What is it?"

I shrugged. "I'm just surprised you can keep up with me. I am a yokai after all."

"You are right; a yokai should be doing better. Maybe you have been slacking off at the Inari shrine."

I stuck my tongue out at him and he laughed. A human like him shouldn't get under my skin, yet he did. "Baka, I'm just slowing down so you can keep up with me. If I was on my own, then I would have already been on the next mountain, if not farther."

"More like you would be on the wrong mountain, heading the wrong way."

"Baka!" I stuck out my tongue again and turned my back on him. Folding my arms, I tried to act like he was a bother, but in reality, I was starting to like his company. Traveling with him made me feel like I belonged again since the other kitsune didn't care to have me around. Yamato didn't seem as bothered and perhaps even enjoyed traveling with me.

Or was he only doing this because Inari told him to? He didn't seem like someone who took orders from anyone. It was one thing to ignore a human request, but it was another to ignore a request from a kami.

So maybe he didn't care about me one way or

another.

I shook my head. No, it wasn't like I cared what he thought, so I tried to push back wondering if he liked me. Humans were fickle, and I despised them.

We spotted a few humans, so I transformed out of my kitsune form. I kept an eye out for them even though I knew there was no way they could have known what I was. Humans didn't attack yokai liked they used to, but the fear was still ingrained in my mind.

We came upon the river and took a break to eat lunch. I sat down on the rock and took my socks and waraji off. Sticking my feet into the water, I felt the refreshing stream cool my body. Yamato took a few things out of his bag.

"What's for lunch?"

"I packed some crackers, cheese, and processed meat. We can have mini sandwiches. If it's not enough, I have more trail mix."

"Trail mix?"

"It's a mix of nuts, dried raisins or berries, and sometimes chocolate. Mine has chocolate."

"That sounds good."

He placed some cheese and meat on a cracker and handed it to me. "Here's one. Let me know how many you want."

I nodded and placed the mini sandwich in my mouth. It was plain, but it filled the stomach. "Can I have four more?"

"Yeah, coming right up."

He quickly made the other sandwiches and handed them to me. I ate them, then jumped down, being careful not to dip my yukata in the water. I tucked the ends in my obi and knelt down to splash my face. I was now refreshed and ready to go.

"Let's go!"

I turned to find Yamato still sitting on the rock, eating.

"You know, I had to make your food, so I'm still eating."

I sighed. "Fine, whatever. I guess I can wait."

"Well, otherwise you will get lost."

I rolled my eyes. "I wouldn't get that lost."

"Sure."

After Yamato finished up eating, we headed back up the mountain. The day went on as usual, with no yokai disturbances. It surprised me we didn't come across any, and I wondered if it was because there were more humans here than I thought would be traveling.

The sun was beginning to set, and we had made our way to the top of Mount Tate. Just as he did the night before, Yamato unpacked his tent and prepared dinner. We had another helping of soup, and after we finished, I stared up at the stars. The night sky was clear, and it had been quite a while since I had seen the stars so bright. I could even see the white river of heaven. Yamato finished cleaning his gear and lay down beside me.

"A beautiful night, isn't it?" Yamato moved some of his bleached hair out of his eyes.

"That it is."

"In the city, you can't see the sky that easily. I always enjoyed coming out into the country or mountains so I can just look up and see the stars."

"Aki-chan and I used to lie out and watch the stars." I grabbed my magatama and held it up. "Sometimes when I look up at the moon, I can see him still. But then I realize he's not there."

"What is that you are holding?"

"Oh this? It's a magatama. Aki-chan gave it to me and said that Susanoo-sama created it and gave it to his sister to be distributed among the gods. He wanted me to always have it so he could always find me."

He was silent, as if not sure what to say.

"But I guess he hasn't wanted to."

"You don't know that. It could have been something else. We will find him and we will know."

I nodded. "Yeah, that sounds good. But I worry…"

Yamato glanced over. "About what?"

"That he doesn't want me anymore. I mean, why else would he leave me like that?"

"He probably had something else going on that he didn't want to have you be involved with." Yamato grabbed my hand. "Don't worry, we will figure it out."

I blushed and pulled my hand away. "You are just a human; you don't understand."

"But I—"

"No. Just because you differ from other humans and can see yokai doesn't mean you belong in my world or understand my pain."

"You are right, I don't. But I also don't fit in the human world because of what I can see going on around me. I'm an outcast no matter where I look. Thank you for clearing that up."

I didn't know how to respond. I never thought about it that way. He really didn't feel he fit in anywhere, which was the reason he lashed out against everything around him. He was smart, he could eventually be someone great, but the problem still stood—he was a delinquent who caused trouble. Or yokai around him caused trouble. It didn't matter as he was always to blame.

"I'm sorry… for what I said," I whispered. "I just… I haven't opened up to a human in a long time, nor have I ever traveled with one. My relationship with them is complicated, and I took it out on you. I am truly sorry about that."

He waved it off. "It's fine. It's not like I don't get it all the time. I don't blame you for my problems. You have your own stuff going on."

I smiled and looked back up at the stars. As the wind blew around, I heard a sound in the distance.

"Chi, chi, chi, chi."

I glanced out in the darkness and noticed a black swarm.

"What is that?" Yamato asked as he leaned up on his forearms.

I stood up and tried to focus on the black mass. It almost appeared as if they were flying. Then it hit me. "Those have to be *yosuzume*."

"They rarely attack humans, right?"

I nodded. "Yes, but that is quite a lot of them…"

"Doesn't the legend say that they indicate if there are wolves nearby?"

My eyes widened, and I searched everywhere I could see, but there was no sign of Akikumo. I took a deep breath. "Isn't the other legend that they signal any yokai are near?"

We both stared at each other in silence as the swarm grew closer. Soon they were right above us, and a few started diving at our heads.

I batted them away with my hand. "Get away from me!"

"Quick!" Yamato gestured. "Get into the tent."

I kept my arms raised as I hurried toward his tent. As I was about to climb in, a yosuzume dove and snatched the magatama out of my hand.

"No! Give it back!"

The yosuzume flew up and away with its group. I darted in the direction they were heading, jumping up and trying to reach the bird. I kept on running, even after hearing Yamato yell my name behind me. I couldn't stop, not when so much was at stake. I would not let some bird take away the one thing that I cared about. I had kept the gift safe for centuries. There was no way I would lose it now.

The birds flew down the mountain toward the tree line, and I raced after them. Luckily I could see them in the dark since I had night vision. As they flew faster, I made a ball of kitsunebi and started throwing it in their direction. They dodged it, which would have been impressive in different circumstances. I screamed at them and as they hit the tree line and scattered through the trees. I lost track of the one that had the magatama.

I collapsed on the ground, tears running down my cheeks. This couldn't be happening, not after all this time. I pounded my fist on the ground. I couldn't believe this. I should have been faster.

"Ketsue-chan!" Yamato came running toward me with his little flashlight. "You shouldn't run off like that! You could have gotten lost! What were you thinking?"

"They stole my necklace. Now I have nothing!"

He stood there, shocked. Then he knelt down and wrapped his arms around me. "We will find him. Don't worry. It will be okay."

I nodded and looked him in the eyes. He was so close, and I started to lean in.

Suddenly I noticed a strange clicking sound, and I

backed away, scanning the area. My heart felt as if it had stopped. I knew that noise, and it was not something I wanted to hear.

CHAPTER TWENTY-TWO

May 1615 (Edo Period)—Nagoya

I slurped up some noodles in my ramen, smiling as it satisfied my stomach. Some drops of broth hit my cheek, but I didn't wipe it away yet, knowing I would spill more. We had just arrived at Nagoya. It wasn't as big as Edo, but I was happy about that. Our time in Edo stressed me out, and I begged Akikumo to not go back for a while. So far, he had agreed, but I doubt that would last for too long.

Akikumo had some business in this town, and

although I didn't enjoy staying in a human town, it was nice to finally stop somewhere for a bit. I was getting tired of how much we moved, even though I enjoyed every bit of it. I wished we could stay still longer, but not in human territory. There were some yokai areas we could be in, who had really good food.

I took a bite of the kimchi toppings, surprised by the intense flavor. It was hot and felt as if my mouth were on fire. I turned to Akikumo, my eyes wide.

He chuckled. "It is hot, isn't it? You can dilute it in the broth a little."

I nodded and moved the kimchi around in my broth. I took another bite, and it was just a little less hot but more manageable. That, or I had gotten used to it.

Akikumo slurped some broth from the bowl. "Humans are getting better at cooking, aren't they?"

I smiled. "Yes!"

"So maybe you will agree that humans are better than you thought they were."

I frowned. Just because they could cook didn't mean they were better overall. Humans still fought, still destroyed everything they didn't understand, and would turn their backs on us yokai. No, having good food didn't show that they were changing—they just liked to have the finer things in life.

I didn't reply to Akikumo and played with the noodles. He wouldn't like what I had to say about humans. We ate our food in silence, and soon there was only broth left. Akikumo and I started sipping the broth from our bowls, bringing it up to our mouths, when his eyes widened and he dropped the bowl. Hostesses rushed over with a rag to help clean up, but it didn't seem like Akikumo noticed them. He placed his hand on his chest as if he were in pain.

"What's wrong?" I asked as he stood up.

"We need to get to Osaka at once." He handed a coin to the owner of the restaurant, and I followed him out into the street. I had never seen Akikumo so frantic like that. His movements weren't as soft or fluid but rushed as if he couldn't focus.

He ran up to a person with a horse. "I can give you this many coins for this horse."

The man saw Akikumo's hand full of coins and nodded. "She's yours. She just got some water and food and should be good to go."

Akikumo nodded and gestured for me to get on the horse with him. I obeyed, and he made the horse start galloping.

"What is wrong?" I asked over the sound of the horse's hooves on the ground below us.

"I have an unpleasant feeling and I need to find something out quickly, although I am afraid it will take a couple of days."

"Where are we going?"

"Osaka. Otousan is there and I am afraid…" He shook his head. "I just need to make sure of something. Don't worry, all right?"

I couldn't help but worry when Akikumo never seemed to worry like this. Something bad had to have happened to Yamiyo, but he was afraid to tell me. Perhaps he was only injured, or perhaps it was something else. I prayed to the kami that he was fine and would be laughing at us in Osaka.

As Akikumo predicted, it took us two days to reach Osaka. We arrived there late at night on the second day of travel to find the castle up in flames. I gasped as the red and orange light reminded me of my home the night my parents died. It was as if I were reliving it once again. My breathing quickened, and yet I felt like I couldn't take in any air. Akikumo noticed and helped me off the horse.

"Ketsue-chan, slow breaths. It is okay; you have me here."

I nodded quickly and slowed down my breathing. I was okay—I was safe. No one was attacking me. All of that happened a long time ago.

"I need you to do me a favor. Can you stay here for me while I search for Yami?"

My eyes widened. He was going to leave me? He said he wouldn't. I couldn't be alone in this area. There were samurai with swords, still fighting each other in the distance, and the stench of blood filled the air. I started hyperventilating again.

"Please calm down. I know you will be safe. You can make it through this, but my otouto needs me. And I need you to be safe as well. Do you understand?"

Reluctantly I nodded. He leaned down, putting his hands on my shoulder, and placed his forehead on mine. "Thank you. I will be right back."

Akikumo handed me the reins of the horse and ran toward the building that was on fire. I glanced around at the people running in every direction, afraid as if an army had just destroyed their castle. I gulped, praying that this wouldn't burn up like Kyoto all those years ago.

Humans seemed to pay me no mind as they shoved each other, trying to get away from the roaring fire. Parts of the roof were now collapsing, and smoke blew in my direction. I coughed and gasped for fresh air. I needed to move, but Akikumo told me to stay there. I glanced all around but didn't see any trace of him. Where was he? How long would he be?

But I couldn't stay here. Even the horse was getting antsy.

I covered my nose with the sleeve of my kimono, but it didn't help as my kimono was already infused with smoke. I slowly pulled the reins away from where we stood, keeping an eye in the direction Akikumo had run.

As if my prayers had been answered, I watched as Akikumo hurried over with a large object in his arms. As he got closer, I could make out it was Yamiyo. He had found him. And he didn't look well.

"Ketsue-chan, let's move away from this smoke!"

I nodded and led the horse toward the forest that wasn't too far. It was away from the humans, so they didn't see Yamiyo as he had changed into his okami. The horse found a small pond and drank. She deserved it as she had taken us on a lengthy journey.

Akikumo laid his brother down. Now that I could get

a better look at him, I saw that his hitatare was soaked with blood. He had a deep wound in his stomach. I knelt down.

"Ojisan!"

His eyes flickered open. His skin was a pale color, unlike his normal darker tone. Something was very wrong. "Oh, my little fox. I am sorry."

Akikumo knelt down, grabbing his brother's hand. "You can't do this to me, otouto. You are stronger than this!"

He shook his head. "No, our power is slowly weakening. Don't you feel it? We okami are losing our strength in this world. It is time for us to move on."

Akikumo shook his head. "Please don't, brother, I beg of you."

He handed Akikumo his katana. "Take this with you. Combine it back into your katana, as it should be." Yamiyo looked over at me. "Take care of him, please."

With that Yamiyo's eyes closed and his body shifted into his wolf form. His chest no longer moved. He had taken his last breath.

Akikumo leaned over him and started crying. I had never seen him cry, and I gently wrapped my arms around him. I didn't know what else to do. He shook, as if trying to suppress it all, but I didn't move. He deserved to be angry—he deserved to cry his eyes out for what had happened. Humans had killed his brother —his only kin. If I were him, I would have never forgiven them. There was no reason for Yamiyo to die, and yet he had lost his life in helping them fight. I knew he should have stayed with us. Then we would still be laughing and eating ramen.

My own tears fell on top of Akikumo's kimono, but he didn't seem to move. He held his brother's body for what felt like hours, and I stayed there supporting him. After a while, Akikumo stood up, his eyes and face red and wet with tears.

"Let us take him up to the mountains and give him a proper burial. Help me get his body onto the horse."

I nodded, and we were able to situate Yamiyo's body on top of the horse. Another day went by as we climbed up the nearest mountain and found a suitable spot to bury him. Akikumo and I dug a hole and buried Yamiyo. Akikumo engraved a large rock and moved it over the grave.

We had taken Yamiyo's body into the mountains with us and given him a proper burial. Akikumo clapped his hands together, and we both prayed for his soul. I knew

I would miss Yamiyo, even though we didn't know each other for that long. I enjoyed his company, and he was always smiling. I was glad he could live a long life like his brother, but I knew it could have lasted a lot longer if it weren't for the humans.

After we finished, Akikumo placed his hand on my shoulder. His warmth felt calming to my heart.

"I am sorry you had to see me like this, Ketsue-chan."

I shook my head. "No, you have gone through a lot. You have no need to apologize."

He smiled. "Thank you. Now, before I forget and otouto comes back to haunt me…" Akikumo pulled out Yamiyo's katana and his own. He held them together, and they morphed into one sword. I gasped, as I had seen nothing like it. One half of the blade was a light silver and the other dark, and the handle was blue and red, as if both aspects were still present.

"Yamiyo and I were created to be opposites, sort of like two swords of the same coin or two sides of a katana. This katana was split for us so we would always be connected, but since he is gone, he wanted me to fuse it back."

I nodded, not saying anything as I didn't know what

to add. He had lost his other half, something closer than a brother.

Akikumo looked at me and smiled, even though tears were falling down his eyes. "We are never truly gone; we just move onto a different life. We may still grieve for we will not see each other in this world but keep moving forward so we can see each other in the next."

I didn't understand his words at that moment, and I didn't know if I ever could.

CHAPTER TWENTY-THREE

Present Day—Hida Mountains

I had lost the one thing I possessed of Akikumo's. Even though I was still shaking and not able to process what had just happened, I knew we needed to get out of there. The clicking sound grew louder and louder. There was only one creature that made a noise like that, and it was one that I didn't want to fight. I grabbed Yamato's wrist, ready to run in the opposite direction.

"Run!"

The sound of clacking seemed to be surrounding us. I

listened closely, trying to pinpoint where the noise was coming from. Was there more than one or was it just echoing? I had no idea, and it wasn't something I really wanted to find the answer to.

Deciding that there was no yokai to the left, I pulled Yamato and ran as fast as I could, praying that Yamato could catch up. The odds were that the yokai was faster, but hopefully we ran away before it realized we were there. I was glad I could see in the dark, then Yamato could just follow my steps and not have to worry where to run.

As if we would ever be that lucky.

The creature appeared out of the bushes in front of us and I fell backward, Yamato falling with me. We both quickly got back to our feet, and I formed a kitsunebi.

"What is that?" Yamato stared at the womanly figure that was attached to the body of a centipede. Her face was contorted with black pincers and red buglike eyes. A substance dripped down from her pincers, and I didn't want to find out what it was.

"An *oomukade*. They aren't the kindest yokai in existence."

Yamato backed away slowly. "I've heard of them in stories, but I haven't ever seen one. What do we do?"

"I will make an opening, and you run. I will be okay and find a way out. There honestly isn't anything you can do to fight this creature."

He gulped and nodded. I made my flame larger and larger. I would have to give this my all as this yokai wasn't some weak thing that I could defeat easily. The oomukade weaved back and forth, snarling. Her eyes looked between the two of us, as if preparing to attack. I threw the blue flame straight at her face.

"Run!" I yelled.

Yamato bolted in the opening he found, and I prayed to the kami he would make it out safely. The oomukade turned and appeared as if she was going to go after him. I leaped in front of her.

"Not so fast! You aren't done dealing with me yet!"

The oomukade snarled as she lunged at me, pincers wide and ready to bite. I jumped back and threw another flame at her. Her body weaved around the trees and bushes. I felt as if she was surrounding me now.

"Kuso…"

Suddenly the body of the oomukade moved toward me in every direction. She was wrapped around me, and I struggled to move and breathe. I tried to use my flame, but it didn't work as I couldn't move my hands.

"Well, well. What do we have here?" The oomukade leaned in, her face close to mine. She was a lot more grotesque than I could see earlier. Her pincers were covered in blood, and her skin was a gray color that shouldn't be a skin tone. Her breath reeked of rotting flesh, smelling worse than miasma, and I didn't want to even look in her eyes.

"Let me go!"

Her pincers clacked together as she laughed. "And let a kitsune go? I am not stupid. Besides, you are the daughter of Akikumo-sama are you not?"

I narrowed my eyes. "What do you know of Akikumo?"

"I know that Akikumo-sama used to rule over these mountains, but now he's weak and cannot stop us. I also remember a certain kitsune who would tag along with him. He would go forward and destroy all yokai that stood in their path to protect her. He was ruthless."

My eyes widened. I had no idea he had done that. He wasn't one who resorted to violence, at least not that I had seen. But he did used to leave me in a spot while he looked for what he said was the right path. Was this what he really was doing? This was a side of him I never knew.

"But it does not matter as today I will kill the one thing that was precious to him. I don't care if he is gone, I will still be satisfied!"

I shook my head. "Akikumo is not gone! He is still alive! I can feel it!"

The oomukade laughed again, her pincers clacking away. "That wolf is long gone. There is no way he is alive—he has not come down this mountain for decades. Now yokai roam freely around, attacking any that stray into our paths. If he was alive, he would have stopped this long ago."

"You are wrong! There is something else going on, I just know it! He wouldn't have died without me knowing!"

"It doesn't matter either way, as you will die now!"

The oomukade grabbed my hair with her hands and opened her mouth. I shut my eyes and screamed. This was the end for me. I would never find Akikumo—I would never receive my ninth tail—I wouldn't know if Yamato was safe.

This was all my fault. I should have stayed at the camp. I should have kept my pendant on and none of this would have happened.

Suddenly the oomukade screamed. I opened my eyes

to find Yamato slicing at the oomukade with a katana. The oomukade loosened her grip around my body, and I leaped out of her control. Creating flame after flame, I sent kitsunebi down at her face. She let out another bloodcurdling scream.

Landing down on the ground, I grabbed Yamato's wrist and started running. As we raced through the forest, I could hear the yokai following us. Why wouldn't she just leave us alone?

"Get back here, kitsune! You will die tonight! I will not let you leave this mountain alive!"

I started running even faster than I thought possible. My legs ached, but I knew if I stopped, we would be dead meat. I didn't have enough time to stop and throw flames in worry that they wouldn't work. No, this creature wanted me dead and would stop at nothing.

What was I going to do?

Whether or not it was an answer, we came upon the end of the forest and the edge of a cliff looking over a deep river. Without thinking, I shoved Yamato off the cliff and jumped down myself, turning around in midair so I could send kitsunebi back at the oomukade who looked down at us. She screamed as it hit her and ran back into the forest.

"I will get you back for this, kitsune!"

I smiled, satisfied I survived against her. Now the new task at hand: the water.

I hit the surface of the river, which hurt more than I thought it would. The water was freezing, as it was the runoff from the snow. We would need to build a fire to warm up and not get sick, or worse. I swam back to the surface and scanned the area for Yamato.

"Yamato?" I called out. A moment later he surfaced. "Oh thank the kami. Are you okay?"

He nodded. "Yeah. For the most part."

I swam over to him. I wondered how deep this river was, as my feet never touched the ground and it was too dark to be able to see the bottom. I noticed the katana still in Yamato's hands.

"Where did you get the katana?"

He held the sword up. I was glad he still had it as it looked oddly familiar. "It was just leaning against a tree. I grabbed it and ran back to help you."

"Let me see it."

He handed it to me and I examined it. It was two colors, as if it had been cut down the middle. The sheath was black and gold, and the handle was red and blue. I would open it later to see if my hunch was correct—this was Akikumo's katana. But if that was the case, why was it out in the open? Akikumo wouldn't have left it somewhere like that.

I looked back up at Yamato. He had risked his life after finding this sword and came back to help me. If it weren't for him, the yokai would have killed me. I never expected a human to ever risk their life for another, especially for me. "Thank you. I would have been dead if you hadn't come back."

Yamato smiled, as if it had been nothing. "It makes us even then."

We started swimming toward the edge when suddenly Yamato disappeared into the dark water.

"Yamato?"

I swam over to where he was but saw no sign of him.

"Yama—" I felt something grab my leg, and I was quickly pulled under as well.

CHAPTER TWENTY-FOUR

Late autumn 1710 (Edo Period)—Edo

We were back in the city I didn't care for. It had been a century since we last entered Edo, and it kept on growing. Now there were checkpoints all along the roads, making sure people didn't cause problems. Each time the guards searched us, however, they never noticed Akikumo's katana. I wished he could make me disappear so I wouldn't have to worry about accidentally transforming, but I knew that wouldn't happen. He wanted me to fit in and mingle with these humans. I hated it and didn't care to know any of them. It wasn't like they would ever care about me if they knew the truth, so why should I change?

I walked beside Akikumo, now coming up to his shoulder. I had four of my tails now and was well into what humans would consider to be my teen years. I would stay in this age range until I had all nine of my tails. I was almost halfway there and couldn't wait. I wondered what adventures I would have with Akikumo then. I would be almost as powerful as him, and I bet we could get in all sorts of trouble.

That thought made me smile, and I fiddled with the pendant Akikumo had given me decades before. As I recalled the memory, I felt Akikumo glance over at me. "What's so funny?"

I shook my head. "Nothing. I was just thinking about when I will get all nine of my tails and how much trouble we will cause. I can't wait to grow up."

Akikumo said nothing, and as I looked over, I found a bit of sorrow in his smile. "What is it?"

"Don't worry about it. I am looking forward to seeing you grow up, that's all. But as for now, we will enjoy the present. Remember Ketsue-chan, it is important to have balance in understanding the past, enjoying the present, and preparing for the future."

I kicked a rock with my waraji. "Yeah, I know. I'm just excited."

"And I am happy you want to grow up. But also enjoy your youth. This is the time of learning for you. Then, when you are an adult, you will also learn a lot more and have many more experiences."

"You like learning, don't you? Is there ever going to be a time when one doesn't have to find more knowledge?"

He shook his head. "No. I believe humans, kami, and yokai alike need to adapt to the times. If you don't keep your mind sharp, you will be whisked away and time won't care."

"Wow. Harsh." I tossed my braided black and red hair back.

"Well, it is true. Look at Japan. It keeps moving forward, and so do we."

I knew he had a point, but I really didn't like how much these humans changed. It wasn't fair for creatures like us who moved more slowly and had longer lives. We were always adapting.

We came upon the gates to Edo and went through the routine questions and pat-down searches. As it had before, the area reeked of a thick miasma. I wrinkled my nose, wishing we were back in the mountains. But it was autumn now, and the snow was beginning to fall in the mountains, so we had moved somewhere warmer. The sky was now dark since the sun had set. Clouds above threatened to rain, and I prayed they would keep on moving and leave my poor hair and kimono alone. At least we were in a city now and could take cover easier.

As we made our way through the streets, I noticed a bunch of people crowding near the shrine, and there were small structures with a line of outdoor signs.

"What is all this?" I asked Akikumo as I clung to his yellow kimono, a little taken aback from the crowds. There were booths as far as the eye could see with humans holding food, fans, and clothing articles they had just bought. The place was crowded, and it was definitely somewhere I didn't want to be right now. The sky was dark, but red paper lanterns lined the area, bringing enough light to the ground that even humans could see. I could hear drums in the distance.

He chuckled. "Has it been that long since I have taken you to a matsuri? I must be one sad excuse as a mentor."

"No, you aren't; you just get sidetracked a lot. And I don't enjoy going to these human areas." I glanced around at all the humans dressed up in their most decorative kimonos. "I don't trust them."

Akikumo patted my shoulder. "You have much to learn, Ketsue-chan. Humans, I admit, can be fickle, but you must not always think so lowly of them. They have built so much in a short amount of time. To us immortal beings, it is fascinating."

I glanced around. I had to admit, so much had changed since I first started journeying with Akikumo. It felt just like yesterday when I was running for my life and trying to destroy any human I saw. Then Akikumo saved me and adopted me in a sense. We have traveled all of Japan ten times over. It didn't feel like much time had passed, and yet humans had grown their cities, had countless battles, and have had generations of children pass. Why were humans so different from us yokai and kami? Why did they not understand life like we did? Why were they always changing?

As for the kami, nothing has changed for them. We always do the same things with them—meeting in October and going over the different prayers. The only thing that has changed was that there appeared to be fewer people praying to the shrines, and kami are being forgotten. Even last week, we had lost one kami—her spirit becoming an eternal cherry tree. It was said that a white snake lives on that tree, never wanting to leave his master. I felt bad for the snake, as he had no one else to believe in.

"I don't understand what you mean by immortal, Aki-chan. Don't kami die when people stop believing in them?"

"They don't die so much as they turn into another form. Their spirit will always live on in the world even if we don't get to physically interact with them. Just like with Yamiyo. When I look up at the starry night, I still feel his spirit watching me."

I looked up at the inky sky. All I could see was black and some shining stars where the clouds had parted. The moon was full, and I could see the rabbits making mochi on the moon. Even with all of that, however, I didn't see Yamiyo anywhere.

"Have you been drinking too much sake again, Aki-chan? I don't see ojisan anywhere."

He laughed. "I am glad you are around to bring me a splendid laugh. You will understand what I mean one day. As for now, let us stop here and enjoy this matsuri?

Then tomorrow we can head south."

I let out a sigh. "Fine. I guess we can see what this is all about. But I expect you to buy me a lot of food."

"Of course."

He grabbed my hand, and we headed toward the crowded area. I didn't feel comfortable around this many humans, but since they were distracted with all the things going on, they wouldn't notice me at all. Then there was the fact that I didn't accidentally turn into my kitsune or fox form anymore.

I noticed that there were quite a few people wearing masks of all different sorts. Some were white and almost comical while others were red and rather scary-looking. As I wandered around, I noticed that some people wearing masks were in fact not human. I stayed closer to Akikumo, afraid what they might be.

"Aki-chan…"

"Don't worry about them. They are just like you and me and traveling around. Would you also like a mask?"

I debated on it, but many humans that appeared the same age as I did were wearing masks. "Sure."

Akikumo led us to a small booth that had multiple types of masks for sale. I looked around and found one that was a fox face. I pointed at it. "That one!"

"Of course." He asked the human for that mask and one mask for himself. I laughed as he put it on.

"What do you think? Do I look frightening?"

"No, you look funny, Aki-chan."

"What if I were a real ogre? Then would you be scared?"

"But you are a wolf, not an ogre."

He patted my shoulder. "Never change, Ketsue-chan. You are too funny."

I wasn't sure what that was supposed to mean, but before I had a chance to ask, I smelled food.

"Can we get some food now?"

"Yes we can."

We got in line for *takoyaki* and ordered as much as I could hold. I chomped on them as we went to the next booth that served fried rice. I kept eating and going to the next booth for a while, Akikumo watching in amazement as I chowed down.

"For someone who doesn't like humans, you sure like their food."

I stuck my tongue out at him. "I believe humans are only good for their cooking. It was the kami, after all, who taught them how."

"That is fair." Akikumo turned as the sound of drums

vibrated through the festival. "Come, let us go watch the performance. I promise it will be spectacular."

I followed Akikumo as I munched on my last onigiri. A bunch of people were all huddled together near a group of men who stood at some large drums. Only one played, repeating parts of a song. His determination dripped off him just like the sweat that fell down his skin. After he finished, another man stepped up and played something similar but not quite the same. I pulled on his sleeve.

"What's going on? Why are they playing by themselves and changing the song?"

"This song is like a battle. Everyone here knows all the parts, and the challenge is to mix it up different from the people before them. It goes on until they decide to stop or people give up."

"Oh," I commented as I turned back to watch. These men were giving it their all, wanting to not only outdo each other but to play around and have fun. Their laughter and determination was fun, and it was hard not to join in and clap each round.

Maybe Akikumo was right—humans knew how to enjoy the moment.

CHAPTER TWENTY-FIVE

Present day—Hida Mountains

I couldn't breathe.

Whatever had grabbed us was pulling us through the water fast. I had no idea which way was up or which way was down. All I knew was I needed to find air, and I needed to save Yamato.

The water was cold—almost like ice as it was filled with the melted snow coming down from the mountains. Once we get out of here—if we got out of here—we would have to find somewhere to warm up, which wouldn't be easy. It was cold out on the mountain, and we'd left a lot of our supplies at the campsite. At that point, I had no idea where we were and I doubted Yamato knew either. I could warm up in my fox form, but Yamato didn't have that luxury. At least I could make a fire with my kitsunebi.

But first I needed to get out of the river.

I tried to look all around, but all I could see was darkness. Whatever had me, had its fingers around my ankle. I could feel its claws piercing my skin and my blood becoming one with the river. Where was it taking me? Or was it trying to drown me and then devour me? Yokai like this made no sense.

I didn't have much longer before I would suffocate or drown. It took all my strength not to inhale the water and keep my hand around the katana. If I was struggling, there was no way that Yamato could last any longer. I had to do something.

Focusing all my might, I tried to form a kitsunebi. It seemed impossible as water extinguished fire. But Akikumo had taught me that my kitsunebi could survive in any environment, no matter what it was. He tried to teach me to use it in the water, but I had never succeeded. Then once I had arrived at the shrine, I didn't want others to see my struggle, and I hadn't tried again.

But if I didn't do it, then Yamato and I would die.

I closed my eyes and focused on my ki. I could do this if I just focused. Kitsunebi was just my ki, and ki could be controlled underwater.

Doubt filled my mind as I didn't feel my hand light up with the flame. I shook my head. No, I wouldn't let it. I had lost so much already. I couldn't lose another friend.

I held out my hand again and focused all my ki. Then I felt the spark of a flame. It was possible. I could do this. I opened my eyes and willed a bigger flame. With the light of the flame, I could now see all around. Yamato was just ahead of me, so it would be easy to hit both of the grotesque, half-fish, half-human creatures that had grabbed us.

Willing it larger and larger, I let the flame go straight at both yokai. An ear-piercing scream echoed through the water as the creatures left us and swam deeper into the river. I swam to Yamato and took us up to the surface.

I gasped for air, but Yamato didn't seem to be moving. I quickly swam over to the shore and laid him down. His chest wasn't moving.

"Kuso…"

Putting my ear to his chest, I listened for a heartbeat. It was faint, but I could still hear it. Since healing was part of being a kitsune at the Inari shrine, I had learned from Ichika how to give CPR.

I pressed on his chest a few times to get the water out of his lungs, then moved to his mouth. I hesitated, feeling a bit weird putting my lips against his but didn't give it a second thought. I blew a few times into his mouth and then pressed against his chest again. Suddenly he reacted and water came shooting out of his mouth. He coughed and turned, gasping for air. He was still alive. I collapsed down, tears forming in my eyes. I had been so scared that I couldn't quite process it all. What would Inari have thought if I had let him die? What about the priest? That is, if I could even leave this mountain.

Yamato bent over, still coughing. "What happened?"

I leaned up and looked at him, shrugging. "Some river yokai grabbed us and tried to drown us. Luckily I was able to use my kitsunebi to scare them off. Then I pulled you back here and gave you CPR." I wrapped my arms around him. "I am so glad you are all right. I was so worried!"

He seemed to hesitate and then wrapped his arms around me. "I'm sorry to have made you worry."

I shook my head. "No, it was all my fault. I shouldn't have run after that yosuzume. This is all our fault, and we almost died because of it."

He shook his head. "No, I have a feeling that oomukade would have found us eventually. She seemed to have been looking for you."

I backed away and looked at him straight in the face. "Still… it attacked us because of me…"

He shrugged. "It's not really your fault. They seem more to have a grudge with Akikumo than you. Once we find him, we will get answers."

I nodded. "Yeah, I suppose you are right."

He leaned over and kissed my cheek. I felt them instantly turn red as my eyes widened. "What was that for?"

"For saving me. Thank you."

I looked away. It was probably just a gesture humans did when thanking someone, and I didn't want him to see my face turn red. "No problem. I didn't want to explain to Inari-sama how I lost you. That's all."

"I see."

We were quiet for a moment, when Yamato brought the conversation back around. "You said you used your kitsunebi underwater? How is that possible? Kitsunebi is supposed to not work underwater, at least that's what the stories say."

I cursed under my breath. "I knew it! He lied to me, that stupid wolf."

Yamato laughed. "I guess if your mentor told you it was possible, then you can do anything, can't you Ketsue-chan?"

I laughed as well. "Yeah, I suppose you are right. I guess that is why I know I will never give up on him. He has to be alive somewhere."

Yamato grabbed my hand. "I agree. And we will find him, I guarantee you that."

I got up and started searching for some firewood. Yamato joined me, but I could tell he was shivering uncontrollably as the wind was cool and felt icy against my wet clothes.

"You can sit while I find some firewood. You have been through a lot and need to warm up."

He nodded and sat back down on the ground. I was able to find some firewood in no time and made an enormous fire so we could warm up faster. As Yamato huddled near the fire, peeling off all his clothes except his underwear to dry, I took off my own and transformed into my fox form. I shook off all the rest of the water and transformed back. Soon our clothes and hair were almost dry, and I sat down and used my power to make the fire more tolerable, as it was burning my skin. I wanted to dry our clothes off more but knew I couldn't keep the fire sustained like that for long before it went out of control. Akikumo would not be happy if I burned down the entire mountain.

As we sat there, I glanced over to find Yamato smiling, even after everything we had experienced.

"What is it?" I asked as we snacked on some of the food that had been protected in plastic that Yamato found in his pocket.

"It's just surprising how strong you are. I mean, I know kitsune are strong, but they should be at a disadvantage underwater. You just amaze me, is all."

I blushed and looked back at the fire. "Well, don't tell everything to your father or Ichika-sama. I don't want them to know how much danger I put you in."

He laughed. "I promise. But I would think you would want them to know about your amazing feats."

I shrugged. "I don't particularly want to go back to

the shrine. I want to find Aki-chan and go on adventuring with him. We used to explore all of Japan, just him and me. I have seen more of this country than would be possible for a human."

"And yet you don't know your way through this mountain."

"Because this world is always changing! Trees change, humans muck up the land, and everything looks so different, not to mention the yokai that have taken over this mountain."

I recalled what the oomukade had said about Akikumo being gone and that's why there were so many yokai. I agreed his power had kept a lot of yokai away from many areas, and he dissipated any miasma that came up in natural areas, so it should have been impossible for the yokai to be on his mountain. Why were they here? Was Akikumo getting weak?

Or was he not on this mountain?

"What's wrong?" Yamato asked.

I shook my head. "It's nothing. We should get some sleep. I have no idea where on the mountain we are, and we will need to gain some altitude to take a look around."

He nodded and lay down in the soft grass. We would

have to find our campsite in the morning and gather our things. I grabbed the katana and unsheathed it. As I had expected—the blade was a dark gray on one side and a light gray on the other side. This was Akikumo's katana. What was it doing in the middle of the forest? Did that mean he was near? It was still in pristine condition, so it couldn't have been left out for that long. How did it get there?

Shaking my head, I put the katana away. At least now I had one thing of his, as I had lost my magatama. I was so stupid for losing that—I should have been more careful. I took a deep breath and tried not to think about it.

I lay down on the grass and looked up at the stars. It had been so long since I had simply looked up and enjoyed them.

"Aki-chan," I whispered. "Are you out there?"

CHAPTER TWENTY-SIX

Summer 1806 (Edo Period)—Hida Mountains

The moon was dark, and the stars lit up the sky like tiny candles, sparkling for what seemed like an eternity. They never seemed to stop as every time I looked up ever since I could remember, they were always there.

I lay next to Akikumo, both our tails swishing lightly on the grass as we enjoyed the view of the universe. The air was cool but not too cold where I felt I needed to transfer into my fox form to stay warm. The ground was warm as well from the sun shining on it all day.

The softness of it made me smile as I could have lain there for hours. I took in a deep breath of the crisp mountain air, catching a bit of the sandalwood and jasmine scent from Akikumo. I understood why he loved it up here. It was far from any human corruption, and one could enjoy nature at its finest. The wind was soft, unlike some nights when the air felt like it was going to war with us. It would howl through the mountainside. I didn't like it, but Akikumo always seemed to love the wind. I wondered if it was because it sounded like wolves howling.

Glancing over at Akikumo, I found him gazing at the sky with a sad smile. I wished I knew what he was thinking as every time he looked up in the night sky, he had the same expression on his face. It was a look of longing, as if he wanted to be up there in the sky as well.

"Do you see your brother up there still, Aki-chan?"

He was silent for a moment, as if still taking in the beauty. "Of course. I see all the loved ones I have ever known up there watching me."

I looked up at the sky. All I could see were stars and darkness. I looked around, wondering if I could pinpoint anyone I knew, but found nothing. I knew he could hear better than me, but could he see better than me as well? "I still don't see them. Where are they?"

He laughed as he raised his hand to point. "You see those group of stars? If you squint ever so slightly, you can make out a wolf. That is my otouto, Yamiyo."

I looked where he was pointing and squinted. "Yeah, I kind of see it. But weren't those stars always there? Before he died?"

Akikumo dropped his hand. "I suppose they were, but I can still tell it's my brother watching over me. Perhaps even your parents are up there, watching over you."

I turned to him. "You think so?"

He nodded. "I know so."

I looked back up, searching all around for them. It had been so long since I had seen them. Would I recognize them? I looked at each and every star, but I saw no trace of them. There weren't new stars up there, and I didn't see their faces. "I feel like you are making this up."

"I am not. Above us is where the heavens lie, and in that is the netherworld. It is both here and not, just like those who have passed. It's a place one can only go to after they die and never return except in the thoughts of others. It is our actions in this world that bring those spirits honor so they can rest."

I tried to put together what Akikumo had said. If they were in the netherworld, then how come what we did in this life mattered to them? Why would they even care about us enough to want us to live for them? Did this life matter to the world of the dead? It made little sense —what did this have to do with the stars?

And I thought the netherworld was where some yokai lived? All of this was rather confusing. But I tried to focus on just one bit of it.

"What are the stars in the sky?" I asked. "How did they get there?"

Akikumo turned to face me, leaning on his arm. "Well, a long, long time ago, when the world was being formed, there was only darkness."

"Was that when you were alive?"

He laughed. "No, that wasn't when I was alive. I'm not that old…"

I shrugged.

"Anyway… Light began to form and moved up and up, forming the stars. Then, particles that were moving but not as fast as the stars settled in the middle and made up the heavens. This was called *Takamagahara*.

Below it, in just darkness, was Earth."

"Which is where we are, right?"

"Yes, that is where we are. Then, on this world, gods began to spontaneously form."

"Including you?"

He sighed. "How old do you think I am?"

"Very old."

He leaned over and started tickling me.

"Stop! Stop! I'm sorry! I will stop talking until you are done!"

Akikumo stopped tickling me and laughed. "Five gods came into existence and after them another ten. In these ten, during the seventh generation, Izanagi-sama and Izanami-sama were born."

"And they created Japan and gave birth to all the other gods, right?" I asked.

He nodded. "Yes, they did. It was from them I was created, right after Japan and humans were formed. I was to take care of them and make sure they understood their duties and to respect the gods that have created them."

I was silent. So many people had forgotten the gods, even with Akikumo going around and helping them. It didn't help that they seemed to forget the knowledge of each generation as time grew. How could they forget such things when they had books and art and shrines? They even spoke of the stories, some from the heart, and they still didn't believe.

"What happens when they forget us?" I asked.

Akikumo took a deep breath and stared up at the sky. "Then the world will move on, and we shall too. But I don't believe they will ever completely forget. The truth will always be in their hearts, and they will remember us and we shall once again flourish."

I looked back up at the sparkling night. Were humans that trustworthy? Could they really remember us after time went on? I had my doubts, but if Akikumo believed so, then perhaps it was possible one day.

Maybe one day humans would accept the yokai and —maybe—accept me.

CHAPTER TWENTY-SEVEN

Present day—Hida Mountains

My eyes flickered open to find a strange blue light emanating from the katana. I blinked a few times, confused as to why it was doing that. I stood up, transforming into my kitsune form, and stepped over to it. Gently I pulled out the katana from its sheath, and the blue light jumped out. Startled, I fell back. What was this light? And why did it just jump out of the katana like that?

As I focused on the light again, I noticed that it was

simply floating in the air, as if trying to get me to pay attention to it. It was trying to tell me something, but I did not understand what that was.

Glancing over at Yamato, I found him still asleep by the fire. Since I had used my kitsunebi, it would last through the night to keep Yamato warm. Turning back to the light, it seemed to slowly be moving back.

Did it want me to follow it? Should I trust it? We had been attacked by a lot of yokai now—I wasn't sure if it would be an excellent idea to trust it so easily.

But it was from Yamiyo and Akikumo's sword. Maybe it was a sign—maybe it would show me where Akikumo's home was.

Which meant I had no time to waste.

Nodding, I gestured to the light. "Lead the way."

I followed the blue light up the mountainside. Once I left the area with the fire, I felt the crisp night air. It was cool compared to the fire, but I knew I would be fine as I had completely dried off now. I kept glancing back. As long as I could see the fire I had made, I could find my way back. That is, if a yokai didn't run me off the cliff and into the water again.

Shaking my head, I pushed back any thoughts of what had happened. I couldn't be that unlucky again.

There was no way. The yokai had been on the other side of the river and wouldn't have been able to get over here. At least that's what I hoped.

The light led me up the mountainside. My body was tired from all that had happened merely hours before, not to mention having traveled across the mountains. But I kept pushing forward, having to know if my hunch was correct.

As I reached the top of the summit, I found a torii gate. It was in rough shape, and as I inspected it, I knew it had to be the one that used to hide all of Akikumo's homes. How could it have gotten this run-down? He used to keep the torii in such pristine condition. I ran my hand over the rough wood, remembering all the times I had stepped through it. My heart raced. Was I going to see my best friend after all these years?

I stepped through the gate, and a small, simple-styled home with broken shoji stood in front of me. I gasped. It was Akikumo's house. I had found it. I was finally there.

"Aki-chan?" I called out as I stepped around the broken roof tiles and wood pieces. "Aki-chan?"

As I stepped inside, I could tell it was abandoned. Dust covered everything and all the shoji were broken, if not rotten. There were holes in the ceiling, having let in years' worth of rain and snow. The furniture was tipped over, and there were no more kimonos or haori in the closets. He had to have abandoned it long ago.

I sank down onto my knees, tears forming in my eyes. After all this time, he was truly gone. There was no way he would have left this place like this. That meant only one thing.

All those people were right—he had perished.

I slammed my fists on the ground. Why didn't Inari just tell me? Why did Inari send me on this wild-goose chase to be slapped in the face with the truth?

Akikumo was gone.

"This isn't fair! Where are you? Why did you leave me!" I choked out. Snot and tears dampened my face as I fell forward and put my face in my hands. "Why did you leave me?"

"Ketsue-chan?"

I looked up, half expecting Akikumo to be standing there, but it was Yamato.

I wiped away the tears. "Yama-chan… I'm sorry I ran off like that. I thought I saw something, but I guess I was wrong." I glanced around the small building. "I guess I was wrong about everything."

He said nothing as he sat down next to me. I buried my face in my hands again. This wasn't fair—why was I so stupid? Why did I not realize earlier he was gone?

Yamato placed his arm around me as I continued weeping. This was too much to process—it was too much to even accept. I wasn't ready for him to leave this world. I needed to know why he left me at the shrine all those years ago.

"Was this his house?" Yamato ended the silence.

I looked up and glanced around. "Yeah, but it seems decades have past. This must have been the last place he came."

"So you believe he is gone?"

I nodded. "Yes. No one has seen him leave the mountain. He must have come up here to take his last breaths in the place he loved most."

Without me. I didn't understand why he did it without me. Why didn't he let me be at his side? Why was I the last to know?

Taking a deep breath, I stood up. "Help me see if there is anything left. Maybe he left a note or something."

Yamato nodded, but I could tell he had the same thought as I—nothing could have lasted in this abandoned place. It seemed that many yokai had made their way through here. Suddenly it hit me.

"Wait, how did you get through the torii without me?"

He shrugged. "Some strange blue light from the katana led me up here, and I walked through the torii with it. I'm not quite sure why I was transferred, but I was. Maybe it was because I brought the katana with me?" He held it up, and I quickly grabbed it, not realizing I had left it behind. I must have been entranced by the blue light to have not noticed.

After everything that had happened on our trip, it really wasn't that surprising he could make it through the torii. He could see yokai after all. "Whatever, I guess we can stay here tonight and then tomorrow we can try to find our stuff."

"Will you be coming back to the Inari shrine?"

"I... I don't know. I thought I would stay with Aki-chan... but now that isn't possible. I don't know what I want, but I suppose I need to talk to Inari-sama either way."

"Yeah, I'm curious why Inari-sama had us go on this trip. Why couldn't they have just told you?"

"Perhaps they didn't know. Or perhaps it was

something else. I can never tell with the kami."

Searching around some more, I found that there was nothing left. Either this place had nothing to begin with, or someone had come along and taken everything. Taking a deep breath, I sat back down.

"Well, I guess we should rest. Tomorrow we will be a big—"

Suddenly there was a large flash of light and the ground shook as thunder filled the sky. It had been clear just moments ago, and yet now we could hear a storm. Both of us ran to the door and found clouds had covered the night sky. How was this possible?

Then I saw him—an enormous creature that appeared like a tiger-dog but glowed as bright as lightning itself.

It was a *raiju*.

There was no way we could defeat such a being, not to mention it wasn't an evil yokai. It was regarded as sacred, almost like a kami.

Raiju let out a roar and paced back and forth, staring straight at us. It glared with its bright eyes, as if we had done something wrong.

"Why are you here?" I asked. It was clear there was nothing I could do but talk to him. It was the only way we would make it out of here alive.

"I protect these mountains and these ruins. I don't let anyone pass through this torii without facing my wrath. No one will taint the burial place of the most legendary okami in existence. No human is worthy to be here!"

The word burial felt like a stab to my heart. Burial place. "I am the daughter of Akikumo-sama. I deserve to be here."

"Akikumo-sama had no daughter."

"That is incorrect. Besides, I am not a human."

"No, you are a kitsune, one that has sworn herself to Inari-sama. You may live due to your service to a god, but your companion I will not let free. He is a human and should not be here. He must die!"

I screamed as the raiju headed straight toward Yamato. Quickly I pulled out the katana and with one big swoop, the entire area went up in a blue flame. The raiju roared as he ran up in the sky, blue light engulfing him. Thunder clashed all around as he screamed.

The power I used was immense, and as the flamed died down, I felt my ki wither.

Then suddenly everything went black.

CHAPTER TWENTY-EIGHT

Summer 1854 (Edo Period)—Fushimi Inari Taisha, Kyoto

"This is a place where most of your kind resides, Ketsue-chan."

I had never seen so many torii gates lined like those. They stretched on forever. They inscribed each gate with a name. From first glance, it seemed that it was mainly human names. Did they build those? Or did they donate? Or were they all priests who had worked at the shrine? I stared at them in awe, as they contrasted the trees and plants so well.

"The red almost matches your eyes and streak in your hair. And, of course, it matches your name."

I nodded. It seemed to fit me, and I wondered how long we would stay here. I thought it was rather beautiful and was surprised Akikumo had never brought me before, although I had a feeling it was because I didn't want to come back to Kyoto. This city was where my parents were killed and my life had completely changed. I never noticed it before, but I wondered if that was why Akikumo never stayed here—he didn't want to bring up painful memories for me.

Yet now he changed his mind. Why was that? Why were we here?

"So there are more kitsune here, Aki-chan?"

He nodded. "Yes, and you will be able to play with them and learn from them while you are here."

"How long are we staying here?"

He didn't answer and kept his eyes ahead. I didn't like how he ignored my question and was about to push further when a kitsune with orange fur appeared. She had all nine tails, which made me stare in awe. She had been alive for at least a thousand years and was considered a kami to some. She wore a yellow-and-pink floral kimono with a white obi. It was intricate, to say the least, and I wondered how she kept it so clean and crisp. Akikumo purchased many kimonos that were as nice for me, but I always seemed to dirty them on our adventures.

The woman bowed. "Akikumo-sama, it is an honor for you to visit our shrine. I am Ichika, the head kitsune of this shrine. Inari-sama is waiting for you."

Akikumo bowed. "Thank you very much, Ichika-san. I am humbled by your hospitality. I believe that what Inari-sama and I need to discuss may bore Ketsue-chan here. Would it be possible for her to meet some of the kitsune that live here? Her full name is Tsuki Ketsueki."

Ichika nodded. "Yes, my daughter and a few others are currently pounding mochi. Would you like to join and learn?"

I glanced over to Akikumo, who smiled. "That sounds like fun. You should go join them."

I turned to Ichika and nodded. "Yeah, I will join them."

"You can take her, Ichika-san. I know my way to Inari-sama."

Ichika bowed. "As you wish, Akikumo-sama."

Akikumo gave me a hug and kissed the top of my

head. "I will see you later, Ketsue-chan."

I touched the top of my head where he kissed it, a little confused. "See you later, Aki-chan."

He turned and headed up through the torii gates. It had been so long since we had ever split up that I almost felt like I wouldn't see his face again. I watched as he stepped up the path, and eventually he was out of view. My heart sank, even though I knew I would see him later. Why was I feeling like that? Had I really gotten that attached?

I turned to Ichika. "So where are we going?"

"This way. The kitsune like to pound the mochi under an old maple tree on the other side of the mountain. It won't take too long to get to if you follow me."

I nodded. "Thank you, Ichika-sama."

"Well, I am glad to see you understand honorifics. I was beginning to wonder after hearing you give that nickname to Akikumo-sama."

I opened my mouth, not quite sure what to say to her backhanded comment. It was none of her business what I called Akikumo. I had traveled Japan with him and was his best friend. How dare she say that.

Taking a deep breath, I let it slide. We wouldn't be staying here for that long, and I could complain to

Akikumo later. I didn't want to get kicked out and have to deal with humans on my own.

Ichika led me through the forest, and after about ten minutes, we came upon a gigantic maple tree. Under it were five kitsune who seemed to be laughing as they pounded the mochi and added water and turned it. I had seen festivals where humans pounded mochi, but I had never done it before. They all turned when they saw us approach.

My stomach felt as if it was filled with butterflies. I had never talked to any other kitsune before. Would they like me? Would I know what to say?

Glancing around, I found that all of them had at least eight tails. I was indeed the youngest one by far, with only five of my tails. Soon they would all have nine tails and I would just be a young kitsune that wasn't as powerful. But that didn't matter. It wasn't like I would stay.

"Everyone, this is Tsuki-san. She came to the shrine with Akikumo-sama. I expect you to be kind to her and bring her back around for supper. I have other tasks I need to complete." With that, Ichika left me standing there with the five new kitsune.

I bowed. "I am pleased to meet you all. I hope we can

be friends."

A male kitsune with nine orange tails stepped forward. His orange hair was shaggy, but not long. He wore an all-white kimono and obi. He looked majestic, almost like Akikumo as he wore a lot of light colors, but something was different. He didn't have the same calm and welcoming energy like Akikumo did. Glancing around, none of them had that type of energy. They almost looked as if they were sizing me up.

As if I was some kind of prey.

The male fox crossed his arms. "Well, what do we have here?"

"I am Tsuki Ketsueki, but you can call me Ketsueki."

He laughed. "As if we would want to become familiar with you." He waved his hand around. "But I guess I should give you my name so you know who to be respectful toward. I am Daiki. I am one of the oldest kitsune here, besides Ichika-sama. Everything you do has to go through me first."

I frowned. That was not what I expected. I clenched my fist, debating on punching him in his perfect chin, but I knew better. Akikumo would be very disappointed if I didn't at least try to make friends. I took a deep breath. "It is nice to meet you, Daiki-sama."

He laughed. "Very good. You learned your place quickly." He gestured to the white-furred kitsune wearing a blue kimono next to him. "This is Hikaru-san. Next to him is Niko-san and Ichika-sama's daughter, Yuki-san."

Niko was a gray kitsune with a pink kimono and purple obi. Yuki, just like her mother, was an orange-haired kitsune with a green kimono. Both the males had nine tails, but the females had eight.

I bowed again. "It is nice to meet you all."

Niko spat at my feet. "You are a disgusting yako."

My nails were digging into my palms. "What's a yako?" All I figured was that it wasn't very nice.

"A feral fox, just like you." Daiki shoved my collar with his long finger. "I do not understand why an okami like Akikumo-sama would want to keep a yako like you around."

I glared at Daiki. "I am not a yako."

They all laughed. Niko opened her fan and smiled at me. "Any kitsune who isn't raised at this shrine is a yako. You don't know proper manners or even how to wear your kimono properly."

Daiki shoved me again. "And look at her fur. It's disgustingly dirty. Her shoes are covered with filth. She appears as wild as the stories say."

"I am not a yako! I travel all around Japan with Aki-chan, that is why my clothes are dirty. I actually work hard, unlike you all."

They all laughed again. Hikaru put his finger on his chin. "Why, isn't that quite the cutesy name for an okami. How close are you to that ossan?"

I shot him a look. "Don't speak of him with such disrespect! He was the one who found me and raised me since I was very little. I have been with him for centuries. None of you know anything about him."

"Well we know that the okami are disappearing and going extinct. It won't be long now before your beloved okami joins their same fate!"

I stepped forward and punched Hikaru straight in the jaw. I only got one good hit in before the other kitsune grabbed me and held me back.

Hikaru wiped the blood off his chin. He looked at it, then licked it off of his finger. "You will pay for that."

He punched me right in the stomach as the other kitsune laughed. This was pure torture, and I couldn't do anything about it.

I just hoped Akikumo would finish up his meeting soon so we could leave this wretched place.

CHAPTER TWENTY-NINE

Present Day—Hida Mountains

My eyes flickered open to find the moon peeking through the clouds above me. It was strange how much brighter the moon could appear when it shone through the clouds.

I heard whispers and turned to find Yamato kneeling beside me, chanting prayers. Then it hit me—what happened.

I had gone one on one with a raiju. Somehow, using that katana, I was able to stop him. It was as if my flames combined with its power. I felt pretty powerful with it, but it had used up so much of my ki I had passed out. Typical.

And now Yamato thought I was dying again and praying for my safety. It had been so long since someone cared about my safety. Probably no one since Akikumo.

Tears ran down my face. He was gone. My best friend was gone. After all this time—after so many years thinking he would come back for me, I was wrong.

I placed my hand down and felt something on the ground. I grabbed it and held it up in the moonlight. It was Akikumo's magatama. How was this even possible? How could it have been here?

A gentle wind whispered through the area, and I took a deep breath. I could almost smell the sandalwood and jasmine that Akikumo always wore. I looked back up at the stars that shone where the clouds from raiju had now parted.

"I am here. I will always be watching you, Ketsue-chan. Just look up."

More tears ran down my face, and I couldn't help but sob. That was why I never felt that he was gone—it was because he was always above me, watching.

Yamato opened his eyes and hugged me. "Thank the kami you are all right."

"Am I? My best friend is gone. I don't know what to do anymore. I don't want to go back to the shrine with those other kitsune. I only stayed because I thought Aki-chan was coming back when really he was trying to set me free."

Yamato held me tight and didn't say a word while I wept. The sun peeked through the mountaintops when I finally calmed down. It was a new dawn. I took another deep breath and nodded.

"We should go find where our stuff is."

"And then what?" Yamato asked.

I shrugged. "I suppose we should just head back. You need to get back to school, don't you?"

He hesitated. "What if… what if I didn't go back? What if we picked up where Akikumo-sama left off? We could travel Japan, looking for yokai who need help, and ask the gods what they need us to do."

I laughed but realized he wasn't joking. "Are you serious? You are just a human."

"That can see yokai."

"That won't live as long as me, not to mention you

aren't as invincible as I am."

He shrugged. "We will figure it out on the way. Besides, you saw I can use this katana."

Yamato pulled the katana out of the sheath, and for a moment I saw Akikumo and Yamiyo in him. It wasn't possible, was it? For them to be reborn like this? I shook my head to push back the thought.

"Your father would be pissed. Not to mention Ichika-sama."

"We will write them a letter on the way."

I laughed. "Fine, I'll bite. On the way to where?"

He smiled. "To our freedom."

I busted up laughing. There was no way this would work. But the more I laughed, the more I noticed another waft of sandalwood and jasmine. Perhaps it was possible and that was where I needed to be.

And perhaps that was why Inari wanted me to go with Yamato. They knew the outcome.

"Well then, lead the way."

He turned and put the katana back. "Well of course I would lead the way. There was no way we would get far with your sense of direction."

"Baka!" I wrapped my arms around his stomach and lifted him off the ground, making him scream like a little girl. We both left as we went through the torii gate, leaving the last of Akikumo's home behind.

CHAPTER THIRTY

Summer 1854 (Edo Period)—Fushimi Inari Taisha, Kyoto

"Aki-chan!" I called out as I wandered the hallways of the shrine. My side and stomach all hurt, and I could tell I looked a bit disheveled. I took a deep breath, searching for his unique scent, but found nothing. "Aki-chan!"

I rounded a corner to find Inari sitting on the floor, writing in a journal. They had long black hair that was let loose. Their kimono was designed with red butterflies on a black fabric. Since it was summer, they didn't seem to be wearing many layers like kami normally did. They turned and smiled, their features both feminine and masculine. I bowed.

"I am sorry for having disturbed you, Inari-sama."

"That is quite all right. I actually have a message for you from Akikumo-sama."

"Oh?"

They nodded and handed me a letter. I opened and read it.

Dearest Ketsue-chan,

We have been together for a very long time, and I think I have been holding you back from your full potential. This place has everything you need to become a full-fledged kitsune. I hope that someday we will meet again, but I am afraid I am growing weak with the growth of the humans spreading more and more into the wilderness. I will never give up on them though, and I believe there is still good in them and that they will never truly forget us.

I ask that you will one day forgive me for leaving you behind. But I just couldn't tell you in person. I guess I am weak when it comes to you.

I will always have a place for you in my heart. Promise me you will be a good fox and become the strongest kitsune that has ever gained all nine of her tails.

I am proud of you,

-Aki-chan.

Tears streamed down my face as I collapsed to the ground. Inari bent down and held me as I cried. I stayed like that for what felt like hours, and Inari never left my side.

***

Thank you so much for reading! I hope you enjoyed *The Legend of Akikumo*! Please think about leaving a review wherever you read books!

I want to thank everyone who made this novel possible. A big thank you to my editor Anne at Victory Editing for helping with this project. Thank you to Biserka Design for the amazing covers for this book! I love it a lot! Arigatou gozaimashita to Mr. and Mrs. Carruthers for answering my questions about Japan and Japanese word usages. It helped a lot! Thank you to Ari as well as I bugged her about Japanese questions as well. Thank you to my cat Zane for being in my face to help edit. Any mistakes are his fault. Thank you to my favorite werewolf, Kaleb, for coming up with the name Akikumo. I better be your favorite fox. And, lastly, thank you to my husband and parents who are always supporting me.

About the Author

Dani Hoots is a science fiction, fantasy, romance, and young adult author who loves anything with a story. She has a B.S. in Anthropology, a Masters of Urban and Environmental Planning, a Certificate in Novel Writing from Arizona State University, and a BS in Herbal Science from Bastyr University.
Currently she is working on a YA urban fantasy series called Daughter of Hades, a YA urban fantasy series called The Wonderland Chronicles, a historic fantasy vampire series called A World of Vampires, and a YA sci-fi series called Sanshlian Series. She has also started up an indie publishing company called FoxTales Press. She also works with Anthill Studios in creating comics through Antik Comics.
Her hobbies include reading, watching anime, cooking, studying different languages, wire walking, hula hoop, and working with plants. She is also an herbalist and sells her concoctions on FoxCraft Apothecary. She lives

in Phoenix with her husband and visits Seattle often.
Feel free to email her with any questions you might
have!
danihootsauthor@gmail.com